Pompeii Fire

Sharon E. Cathcart

Dedication

For Jim Noble, whose heart was full of courage and love, and for whom traveling the world was such a delight.
Quod memoratur, vivit.

Epigraph

"Who can carry
The incineration of a Universe?"
— Ovid, *Tales from Ovid: 24 Passages from the Metamorphoses*

Prologue

Day 10

Pompeii Archaeological Park

Damiano led the way into the restored gladiator barracks. "I'm sorry you didn't get to see this when you were here before. It was in this room that the two people I told you about were found: a man, chained to the wall, and a woman wearing a good deal of jewelry. There is some speculation that they were lovers, but there were a lot of other people in the *quadriporticus* when the eruption happened. It could just be that she was trying to get out of the city and wound up seeking refuge here."

Stephanie stood outside the cell behind him, her face panic-stricken. "Suetonius*? Ubi Suetonius est?*"

"What?"

"Suetonius!" Tears streamed from Stephanie's eyes as she cried out. "*Ubi Suetonius est*?"

Damiano turned back just in time to catch her as her eyes rolled back in her head.

Why is she asking where Suetonius is? And why is she speaking Latin?

He placed her gently on the stone floor, out of the sun. Then, he called the emergency number to get an ambulance. Of course, the automobile couldn't enter the archaeological park; he needed to coordinate with a worker. Surely the archaeologists on-site could be of some assistance.

As Damiano ran to find either a park attendant or the robotic dog and drone that patrolled the site, all while talking to the emergency operator on his mobile, a large, black and tan mongrel who lived in the ruins trotted over and settled down next to Stephanie. His posture was vigilant; no one would harm her while he was on duty.

CHAPTER 1

SIX MONTHS EARLIER

"You have to submit your portfolio," Raylene Thibodeaux insisted. "You're one of the best travel writers out there. *Time Away* would be lucky to have you."

Stephanie Marlowe's neighbor and best friend was nothing if not persistent. "Just send your samples. If you aren't chosen, you're out nothing but time and a little effort."

Stephanie finally agreed and sent off her resume and clips. If nothing else, the ebullient Raylene would be pacified.

"I've got a feeling about this, Steph." Raylene practically bounded out of the room.

Stephanie wished she had her friend's confidence in the matter; the "Temporary Local" feature had been dark for more than a year while the staff at *Time Away* staff searched for a new columnist.

Stephanie wasn't going to hold her breath.

Especially since success meant leaving the house.

"We were very impressed with your portfolio. I would like to offer you the 'Temporary Local' position. Of course, we've made some changes since the virus, so we won't keep you in the area for a full month like we used to do," Diana Corbett Boudreaux explained. Diana had been promoted to the role of editor some months before. "We'll have you there for two weeks, with an eye toward the human interest aspects of the area alongside the attractions. We're sending you to southern Italy, to stay in the village of Pompei."

Stephanie could hardly believe it. Staff gigs were the exception and not the rule for people in her field; travel writing was a constant round of freelancing and trying to make a name for one's self. Those stories covering art and wine festivals, and three-day weekend activities, had paid off.

"Pompei? Why not Naples proper?" Stephanie was glad it wasn't a video call; she was thrilled to take the column, but not so much about where she was being sent. She hoped that her question wouldn't jeopardize the opportunity.

"Because I want you to stay in the village and cover what it's like to live there. After the coronavirus, I suspect that things will be a lot different. I just have a feeling about this. Besides, your resume says you speak Italian. You might want to take some basic Latin, so you can translate ancient graffiti in the archaeology site, but it's up to you. And really, Naples is not what you'd call a safe place. It has a high crime rate, and Pompei doesn't. We've arranged a hotel room, not far from the local train station. Please say yes."

What Diana didn't say was that there was something magical about the "Temporary Local" feature. Putting the right person in the right place was life-changing, as Diana herself knew. It was how she'd met her husband, Amos, in New Orleans.

Stephanie accepted the assignment gratefully. She couldn't help remembering how miserable she'd been during the San Francisco Bay Area's lockdown. *Bay Area Weekly* had closed its physical office and sent everyone to work from home for the duration. Even with her pretty little two-bedroom house near Ocean Beach, Stephanie felt the pain of being shut in. Naturally introverted, as many writers were, she still relished the opportunity to visit neighborhood restaurants, walk on the beach, go to the nearby San Francisco Zoo, the Cliff House, and more. The pandemic killed both the Cliff House and Louis' Seafood, with their beautiful views and tasty food. Then, *Bay Area Weekly* eliminated her column and she found herself freelancing when and where she could. When the city she loved came slowly back to life, it was as though a weight had lifted from her heart. Even through the second lockdown, she felt hope, ignoring the fear that nibbled around the edges. Leaving the house had become more difficult after that second go-round. Soon, though, the vaccinations came and Stephanie felt her life returning to normal. Surely the same would be true of the people she met in Italy.

She not only brushed up on her Italian, but took an on-line course in Latin “just in case.” She was not sure what good it would do, but it couldn’t hurt. Maybe it would help her get future assignments in the classical world. She’d also read up on Pompeii, watched a number of documentaries on Netflix and YouTube, and felt pretty well prepared for her journey. Research was a crucial part of any travel writer’s process.

What she wasn’t prepared for was how she started dreaming about gladiators. She’d never been one for team sports, and gladiatorial games just seemed like more of the same. Still, there was one gladiator she dreamed of repeatedly. He had a small, round shield over one arm, a short, curved sword in the other hand, bronze shin guards, and a closed helmet: a Thracian, they had called this type of fighter. His chest was smooth and hairless, his skin tanned by the sun, and his musculature that of a man accustomed to hard work. She always seemed to be watching him from a distance, even though in the dreams she knew who he was. Through the helmet’s eye shields, she could tell his eyes were green.

CHAPTER 2

DAY 1

"You're going to have a great time. I want lots of pictures on Instagram!" Raylene put Stephanie's suitcase on the curb outside the airport terminal. "I'm jealous of this adventure."

"I'm going to miss you so much, Raye." Stephanie hugged her friend. "Thanks for the lift. I'll bring you back a souvenir."

"The hell with souvenirs, girl. Bring me back a handsome Italian man!"

Raye's laughter was contagious.

"I'm not going there to find a man," Stephanie replied, "but if someone leaves one lying around, well, who am I to argue with fate? And if not, well, there's always one of your Cajun cousins."

"Heaven knows there are enough of them," Raye laughed. "I lost count years ago. Travel safe!"

The two friends hugged once more, and then Stephanie went into the airport. She hoped Raylene hadn't noticed how badly her hands were shaking.

Stephanie boarded an overnight plane to Paris and, after going through passport control again, caught a flight into Naples. She'd arranged a car and driver to take her to the hotel and was more glad than ever about that decision when they left the airport. It was apparent that traffic rules and regulations went right out the window until one left Naples. She tried to distract herself by looking at the landscape as they passed; her driver pointed out sights like the Isle of Capri, which looked for all the world like a pregnant woman lying down for a nap.

Once she'd unpacked, Stephanie explored the mini-fridge in the hotel room. There were snacks and drinks inside, but the selection was limited. She'd have to find a market soon. The bed looked inviting after the long flights, so she decided to take a nap. Perhaps the gladiator dreams would stop now that she was finally at her destination.

She awoke a couple of hours later, refreshed but hungry. A walk through town and something to eat were high on her agenda. Stephanie dropped her keys off at the desk, walked out the door, and made a right turn at the bottom of the street. A big black and tan dog approached Stephanie as she walked down the *Via Bartolo Lungo* to get a general idea of Pompei's layout and to see where the closest entrance to the ruins might be. He was friendly, wagging his tail, and let Stephanie pet him. The dog's calm presence helped immensely.

"You're a good dog, aren't you? Do you speak English? No? *Buon cane. Buon cane.*" The dog's tail lashed furiously as she spoke to him, and then he picked up speed to trot away.

Stephanie had often thought about getting a dog. Walking a dog on the beach would be a nice way to spend time, and keep her from being lonely. Her last boyfriend had been gone a while, having moved to a less costly area; she could use the company. Raye had been talking about going back to New Orleans for ages as well. Maybe working from home wouldn't be so bad with a nice dog for company. Raylene was after her to be more sociable; walking a dog at Fort Funston would be a good way to meet new people, too. And, a dog would mean she had to go out. Something to file away for future consideration.

She continued down the way, looking in the windows of the souvenir shops and reading restaurant menus to decide what to eat.

Damiano De Luca tried not to flinch as the barber grabbed the soft sweep of his fringe, lifted it, and chopped it off close to his hairline. A bet was a bet, even if it was over football. The wager was simple enough: whoever's team lost would stand outside the amphitheater gate of Pompeii, dressed as a gladiator, for a full day during the university's spring break to raise money to help care for the feral dogs who lived on the archaeology site. Dom took the loss gracefully and then decided if he was going to do a thing, he was going to do it properly. Glad for the time that he spent in the gym, he'd gone to the spa to have everything waxed that an ancient Roman would have had plucked. He thought he'd never get over the pain, but had to admit he liked the effect; his muscles looked like they were carved out of marble. Then he went to his barber and asked for a Caesar haircut, even though he thought he would regret it. A straight-razor shave eliminated the fashionable scruff from his cheeks and chin. He would at least look the part in the morning. Maybe his university classics students would be amused at the photographs his friends promised to take.

When he looked in the barber's mirror, his green eyes seemed more fierce under the now-cropped black waves. Far from looking ridiculous, he looked like a warrior. Just as he'd wanted, but hardly dared hope.

CHAPTER 3
DAY 2

Damiano stood patiently outside the amphitheater gate to the Pompeiian ruins as the tourists posed with him in his borrowed Thracian armor, each dropping a five euro bill into the bucket on the ground next to his helmet. That was when he saw her, waiting among the rest. She wore a sleeveless lavender dress that buttoned down the front all the way to her ankles, yet moved with the breeze. Her feet were clad in those hideous walking sandals that marked her as an American, but at least they would keep her safe on the rough terrain inside the archaeological park. She wore sunglasses, so he couldn't see her eyes. Her hair, pulled back in a ponytail, was brown with golden lights that promised she either spent a lot of time outdoors or in a beauty salon.

Where he had greeted every other visitor as "*signore*" or "*signorina,*" when it was her turn, Damiano called the woman "*principessa.*"

"You wear the purple, so you must be royalty." He held out his hand to her and she placed her palm in it. Even her nails were lavender, with a slight sparkle. He placed her hand against his bare chest; it was clear that both them felt a jolt of connection. Her hand trembled, fluttering against his smooth skin.

Frightened? Why?

"Take off your sunglasses, *principessa*; the photo will be better."

Her eyes were blue, as he had somehow known they would be. After one of the waiting tourists took the photo and returned Stephanie's phone, Damiano expressed concern that she would get a sunburn in the park.

"There is no shade in there, *principessa*."

"It's all right; I bought this scarf yesterday." From her straw handbag she pulled a sheer golden scarf and draped it over her head.

Like a *flammeum*. An ancient wedding veil, just shading her amazing eyes. A chill ran down Damiano's spine

His green eyes held her gaze, and he spoke to her in the old tongue. "*Salve*, Drusilla."

Her response surprised both of them. "*Salve, thraex*." She'd answered in Latin without a second thought; clearly her studies worked.

A man behind them cleared his throat. "Excuse me? Other people are waiting to have their pictures made."

Damiano lifted Stephanie's hand to his lips, which he brushed across her knuckles while still holding her gaze with those arresting green eyes.

"Until we meet again, *principessa.*" He watched her enter the metal detector room and then turned his attention back to the crowds. His mind was elsewhere as laughing tourists surrounded him and made donations for the dogs.

Stephanie couldn't shake the idea that the faux gladiator's green eyes were the same ones she had seen in her dream. She accepted the ticket taker's map and made her way up the road near the amphitheater on her right and the *palaestra* on her left, but she was distracted as she went.

She also couldn't help thinking about the difference between this tourist-attraction gladiator and those she had seen in Rome some years before when she took a trip with friends. He was at least raising funds for a good cause, and looked the part. The men in Rome had barely tried; in one case, the man portraying a centurion wore a sweater and thermal underwear under his *lorica segmentata.* To be fair, it was chilly that day, but it had looked absurd. Plus, it was clear that those tourist gladiators and centurions hanging around the Colosseum were in it for themselves.

This gladiator's body, by contrast, reminded her of statues she'd seen in museums. She remembered how his heartbeat felt under her hand, the warmth of his skin, and realized that she was blushing.

She sat on a raised sidewalk outside the House of Julia Felix and sent the photo of herself and the gorgeous green-eyed man to Raylene. After resting for a few more minutes, she got up to explore more of the ruins.

The same black and tan dog she'd seen the night before was soon trotting along beside her. She petted his head gently, and he seemed content to keep her company.

Damiano walked home, his friend's armor in a bag. He must have had his photograph taken dozens of times that day, and gave nearly 500 euros to the attendants at Pompeii to care for the dogs. He wanted nothing so much as a shower and change of clothes.

He couldn't stop thinking about the woman he'd called princess. She was what his grandmother would have called "*fare bella figura*," a woman who made a good impression, with her nail lacquer matching her dress, and that golden scarf for contrast. His artist's eye always caught the details, and sometimes he wished it didn't. He doubted he'd see her again; another tourist visiting the ruins, and then she'd be gone to Naples, Rome, Sorrento … somewhere that was not his tiny village. Few of the tourists stayed in Pompei beyond their time in the ruins. Damiano was disappointed at the notion of never seeing the American woman again, though he couldn't figure out why.

A shower and a walk will clear my head. He walked a little faster toward home.

Stephanie studied the menu and tried to decide what she wanted. The weather was lovely, so she was at one of the sidewalk tables. Damiano saw her from across the street and hurried over, unable to believe his luck.

"*Principessa*!"

"*Thraex*," she smiled, putting her menu on the table. "My name is Stephanie."

"Damiano, but please call me Dom. You're at my cousin's restaurant! May I join you?"

"That would be lovely." It wouldn't hurt to get some local color for her story, and Damiano was certainly pleasant to look at. He now wore a pale green linen shirt that made his eyes gleam like emeralds, and a pair of snug but well-worn jeans.

"So, what brings you to Pompei? Just the ruins?" He took the chair next to her rather than sitting across the table. "I hope you don't mind, but I assumed it would be easier for you if we spoke English."

"Honestly, I'm grateful. My Italian is okay, but that's as far as it goes. Your English is excellent. I'm here to write a travel article." She dug around in her straw bag and found a business card, which she slid over to him. "It's my first assignment for a new column. I'm supposed to show how the area is recovering, and talk about things for visitors to do."

"Thank you for your kind words; I'm a university professor, so I am proud to be multilingual." He grinned, showing white teeth against his tanned skin. "So, you want to know what it was like for us during the shut-down. Well, I would like to ask you the same thing. First, I will get us something to drink." He stood up and strode through the huge double doors that led to the restaurant's interior. A quick conference with one of the men inside resulted in a bottle being uncorked.

"It was awful," she told Damiano when he came back to the table with two glasses of a local red wine. "I don't know how I would have managed without my neighbor, Raylene. We'd been friends for years, ever since she bought the house next door."

Damiano listened as Stephanie told him about her experiences, not just with the lockdowns that came and went repeatedly, but about how she felt. Among other things, he learned that Stephanie injured one of her knees early on in the pandemic during a walk, and was limited in what she could do.

"Raylene pretty much saved me. For instance, she fixed Easter dinner so that I didn't have to cook after I was hurt, and carried the groceries upstairs for me. After that, she insisted on doing things around the house since I was supposed to be on bedrest. We'd do manicure nights or play cards. I was going stir crazy to begin with, so having a little company helped." Stephanie debated telling Damiano about the agoraphobia; he was so easy to talk to. She decided it was best to not get into too much detail; after all, she'd be gone in two weeks and it wouldn't matter.

"Then, when things started to get better and I couldn't handle going out, she would accompany me on short outings until I felt safe again," Stephanie continued. "How about you?"

"My *nonna* came to stay with me; I didn't want her living alone in Naples. So, I wasn't by myself either. Still, I had to hurry up and figure out how to teach my students by video, and we had to plan everything carefully. We could go out only to the grocery and the pharmacy once per week, and I did all of that so *Nonna* wasn't exposed. I was glad we were here instead of Naples; it's quite crowded there. I also did a small painting project in our home, which gave me something else to think about." He took a sip of the wine. "And now, you are here for your magazine, to tell people it's safe to return?"

"More than that; I'll be writing about all kinds of experiences I have during these two weeks. I want to give people a picture of what it's like to live here." Stephanie tasted the wine. "This is very good."

"I'm glad you like it; we have been making wine here since before Vesuvius erupted. As for living here? I will tell you, *principessa*. It's not always easy. All of these restaurants and shops? They depend more on the tourists than anything else. When the ruins are open and busy, they thrive and they put aside money for the quieter times. In the winter, some restaurants do not open at all, and the ones that do might close a couple of nights a week. This place, in the winter? My cousins tell me that they are lucky to have one party for supper most nights. So, I don't think I need to tell you how hard it was during the lockdowns."

"I can't even imagine." Stephanie picked up her menu again. "What do you recommend?"

"If you will trust me, Stephanie, I will select a few things that are regional specialties."

"That would be wonderful."

Damiano delivered an order to the waiter in Italian so rapid that Stephanie couldn't follow it.

Well, this is supposed to be an adventure. I'll just have to be surprised.

Soon, two steaming plates of *pasta alla genovese* sat in front of them. The oniony sauce with flakes of shredded beef throughout was like nothing Stephanie had ever tasted before. Dessert was a gorgeous lemon olive oil cake, followed by Amaro liqueur as a digestif.

"This was so good," Stephanie said, getting out her expense card. "You must let me pay."

"Nonsense. I told my cousin about you, and he says the meal is on the house. He only asks that, if you speak of his establishment, you do so kindly. May I walk you back to your hotel?"

"That's very nice of you. I'm at the Palma, just around the corner."

When they entered the hotel lobby, Stephanie collected her key from the receptionist, who greeted Damiano with a delighted "*Professore* De Luca! What a pleasure to see you."

"You've been keeping up with your studies, *Signorina* Giusti?"

"I have!" She held up a paperback edition of Ovid's *Metamorphoses*. "I'm looking forward to class being back in session."

Damiano walked Stephanie to the elevator and pushed the call button. "Perhaps, *principessa,* you will let me take you sightseeing tomorrow?"

"I would enjoy that very much. Shall we plan on ten o'clock? We can meet here in the lobby."

"I will count the minutes, *principessa.*"

He watched the elevator make its brief climb, wished his student a good evening, and walked the short way home.

After a chat with his grandmother, Damiano logged on to his computer. Using the information from Stephanie's business card, he quickly found her social media. He was fascinated with her Instagram account. She had shared photos of her knee injury and talked of how it turned into bursitis, doing her nails with a blonde woman who could only be Raylene, and even links to videos of her talking about some of the souvenirs from various trips she'd taken as a travel writer. Her style was friendly and engaging, and it was no wonder that she had so many fans and followers. He particularly liked the videos where she discussed her fondness for pop music from the 1960s and 1970s; it was an unexpected quirk that delighted him. She played songs and sometimes sang along with the records in a smooth alto.

One of the other things he noticed was how easily Stephanie smiled and laughed with her friend.

I would love to paint her. Her face is so engaging. And her hands; I could do a study on them alone. She has no idea how appealing she is, of how she brings viewers into her life in such a way that makes them feel welcomed and safe. I wonder how I could capture that in a portrait. Her smile, perhaps ... or those beautiful blue eyes.

The thing that niggled most at his mind was how familiar she seemed. While it made no sense, Damiano was certain they had met before. His travels to the United States in the past few years before the pandemic were limited to academic conferences rather than leisure travel, which made it less likely. Still, the thought was not readily dismissed.

Damiano had difficulty falling asleep that night; when slumber finally overtook him, his dreams were full of the American woman.

As for Stephanie, she spent some time on the internet looking up *Professore* De Luca to see whether he was who and what he claimed. There, she discovered he was one of the foremost experts on Pompeii, as well a professor of literature at the University of Naples. The “small painting project" he had worked on during the shelter-in-place was an elaborate mural in what she knew from her research to be Third Style painting. He was a gifted artist. His head shot showed him in a tailored jacket and open-collared shirt, his hair longer and perfectly cut, a fashionable crop of stubble on his cheeks.

I would never have been able to pay attention in class if my professors looked like him.

Finally, she phoned Raylene, despite the hour, and told her about how she'd passed her day.

"Wait. That hunky gladiator is a college professor?" Raylene was incredulous. "I would have been a lot more interested in staying in school past community college if my teachers had looked like that."

"I know. He's easy on the eyes, for sure, but probably boring as hell at the end of the day."

"You don't sound like you were bored, Stephanie."

"He was nice, and you know what that means. He'll turn out to be dull as dishwater."

"What it means is that you don't know how to act in a relationship where you're not constantly trying to prove yourself. What would happen if you just let a decent guy be nice to you? Would the world come to an end? Is it possible that you'd get to see some of your own worth?" Raylene sighed. "Look, I've been there, too. I used to chase the bad boys who treated me terribly. I thought I didn't deserve more than that and if I'd just do the perfect thing, be indispensable, they'd stick around and realize how much they loved me. Do you know what happened, every damn time? They left, and I'd be curled up in a ball in the middle of my bed feeling like I was going to throw up. I'd let who I was disappear in order to be who I thought they wanted."

"Okay …" Stephanie wasn't sure where her friend was going with these ideas. She did, however, remember that this was pretty much how her last relationship had ended.

"So, you're there for two weeks. If he turns out to be a louse, you can walk away, but something tells me a guy who teaches classics and raises money to take care of stray dogs is pretty decent. He's taking you sightseeing tomorrow. If it's a horrible, dull experience you don't have to see him again. But I wouldn't throw out the gladiator with the bathwater. Maybe you'll wind up having a vacation romance. Could be just what the doctor ordered."

"I'm not on vacation, Raye."

"You know what I mean."

"Goodnight, Raylene."

"I want to hear how it went, girl. Don't leave me hanging. Sleep well."

CHAPTER 4

DAY 3

The next morning, Damiano was waiting in the lobby when Stephanie came out of the elevator. She wore a loose white shirt over jeans and those same unattractive sandals.

"*Buongiorno, principessa*! I thought perhaps we would go to Sorrento today. We can walk over to my car if you would like, or we can take the train. Unless you would like to do something else, of course."

"That sounds perfect. I would like the drive, I think. We can perhaps talk better than on a crowded train."

She gave her keys to the receptionist and the two of them walked across the plaza.

Stephanie waited for Damiano to pull his car out of a small garage. He parked the car, came around and opened the door for her, and made sure she was comfortable before returning to the driver's seat. Reflecting on her conversation with Raylene, Stephanie realized that she found his old-fashioned manners refreshing.

"I also thought that we might take the boat from Sorrento to Capri if you would like,' Damiano said as he entered the freeway. ''It's beautiful there, and it doesn't take too long."

Stephanie agreed readily.

"It will take about half an hour to get to Sorrento from here, and then the ferry to Capri is about twenty-five minutes," Damiano explained as they drove out of town. "I took the liberty of ordering our tickets last night. I had hoped you would agree, but we can still do something different if you would prefer."

"That's very kind of you. I think that sounds great, and I'm sure my readers will enjoy learning about it."

"I also brought some food. *Nonna* thinks we will starve if we don't take something with us, although there are some restaurants on Capri that are quite good. Still, it is only cheese, bread, fruit and a little wine; we will have room afterward for a *tartufo*."

Stephanie thanked him, and aimed her camera phone out the window to capture images of the coast going by. After a few moments, she put it away.

"Tell me about growing up here," she asked.

Dom spun a tale of Catholic school, a fascination with a past that could not be ignored when one grew up in Pompei, and a determination to better himself. A mother who died of cancer; a father remarried and living in Canada. Undergraduate and post-grad education at the university where he now taught, eventually a doctorate from UC Berkeley ("Almost in your own back yard, *principessa*") and a return to Italy rounded out the story.

"Very few people who leave *Campania* come back," he finished. "That's part of the reason so few people in the region speak English; there's more emigration than immigration. Still, it's a part of the world that gets into your heart and doesn't leave. At least we are still here; there are many villages all over the country that have been completely abandoned."

"No wife and children? I hope that's not too personal."

"No, it's not too personal. To my *nonna*'s disappointment, I have not met the right woman. And you, *principessa*? No husband?"

"No, no husband. And no boyfriend, either. The last one's been gone a while and, to be honest, I don't really miss him."

Dom reached over and took her hand. "Well, if I may be so bold, maybe this is a new day for both of us."

Stephanie had worried about the ferry ride when she considered a trip to Capri; she was not a very good sailor. Even taking friends out on the ferries in San Francisco Bay made her queasy. Luckily, Dom kept her distracted by pointing out sights from the boat that she should capture for her articles and focused her attention away from the horizon as a result. The trip to the island passed far more quickly than she'd thought.

"We should have our lunch at the villas of Tiberius. There is a route that is longer, but a little easier to walk. Before that, though, I want to stop in at a friend's shop."

Dom led Stephanie into a shop with beautiful sandals in the window. She couldn't follow a lot of the rapid-fire Italian that commenced, catching only terms like "*la mia donna*," which meant "my lady," and some negotiations that resulted in Dom handing over his credit card.

"Stand on the paper," the shopkeeper instructed. "Shoes will be ready when you come back."

"What?"

"Take off your shoes, *principessa*, and let him measure your feet. I've ordered some sandals to be made for you. They won't be practical for walking around here, but they will be pretty for town."

Stephanie did as she was asked, and soon they were on a little bus to the ruins of Villa Damecuta.

"Tiberius ruled Rome from here," Dom explained. "He didn't like Rome at all. Here, he could do as he pleased, with whom he pleased. He had twelve villas on Capri, but I chose this one so that you could see the Blue Grotto after we have our lunch. It is only a twenty minute walk from Damecuta. It is a longer walk to Villa Jovis, and I don't want to wear you out."

The views were breathtaking. Dom took lunch from his backpack and spread a cloth on the ground for them to sit on as they looked out over the sea and ate. Stephanie took photos and made some voice memos on her phone so that she could document the experience properly.

Dom laid down on the blanket, resting his head on Stephanie's leg. She stroked his wavy, raven locks as she observed the scenery around them. It all felt natural and comfortable, despite the newness of their acquaintance.

"It's so beautiful, Damiano."

"Indeed, it is." Dom looked at his watch. "Let us gather our things and walk down to the grotto; we will need to hire a row boat to go into the grotto, and you really must see it."

He helped Stephanie to her feet and put their picnic things back in the bag before leading the way down to a narrow jetty.

When they got to the landing, tiny dinghies were taking on tourists two at a time. Dom helped Stephanie down, and the guide began rowing them around the island. Dom pointed out the high limestone cliffs and talked about how they made the island readily defensible.

"This is why it was a favorite place for emperors to come for their holidays, and also why Tiberius decided to just stay here and leave Sejanus in charge of day-to-day matters in Rome. He felt safer. Sejanus did, too; he ruled Rome with an iron hand, since he knew no one would interfere with his ambitions."

When the boat came around to a tiny gap in the cliff wall, with a narrow chain coming out of its entrance and attached to the rocks, Damiano slid down into the boat below the gunwales.

"You will need to lie down, *principessa*. We have to go through that tiny gap and you cannot sit up."

"No, Dom. Just no. I'm claustrophobic; I can't. I didn't know the opening would be this small; please, we have to go back."

"You will be safe, I promise. I will not let any harm come to you. Slide down next to me and put your head on my shoulder."

Stephanie did as he asked, burying her face in his neck. His skin smelled of warm sun and limes; Stephanie breathed in as she closed her eyes and settled against him. Dom held her gently in his arms as the guide grabbed the chain and pulled hard against it to slide the boat through the narrow opening.

"You can sit up now," Dom said. "It's safe."

Stephanie could hardly believe her eyes. Their guide had rowed them in, explaining that this had been part of Tiberius' complex intended to be a special dining room. The sunlight shining on the limestone at the bottom of the lake gave the water a rare shade of blue which, in turn, gave the grotto its name.

"The color is amazing," Stephanie whispered to Dom.

"Not nearly as amazing as your beautiful blue eyes, *principessa*." He put his fingers gently under her chin, and tilted her face toward his; the kiss that followed was both gentle and intoxicating.

Stephanie smiled, her pupils dilated in the semi-darkness of the cave. "I would very much like to do that again."

Dom was happy to oblige. The skipper of the boat sang "*O Sole Mio*" and rowed them around a few times. Stephanie finally gathered her wits and took some photographs before the boat joined a queue of others waiting to go back out to the bay.

When it was time to leave the grotto, Dom once again took Stephanie in his arms and held her while the boat came back through that tiny opening.

Once they were back on land, the two made their way back to the shoemaker's shop where they started the day. The man who had measured Stephanie's feet handed her two slim boxes; she opened the first to find a pair of slim sandals encrusted with blue crystal gems. The second contained a pair made from cork, a local specialty.

"They'll always remind me of my visit to the grotto," she smiled. "Thank you. Both of you. *Mille grazie*."

The shoemaker put the boxes in a bag. As they left the shop, Dom took Stephanie's hand.

"I promised you a *tartufo* before we go home. Come with me."

He led her into an ice cream shop and placed an order. Soon, the two of them were sharing chocolate gelato stuffed with cherries and encrusted with chocolate chips, dipping separate spoons into one treat as though they had been dating forever. They chatted and laughed; Stephanie didn't want the day to end.

"I would like to take you also to the Emerald Grotto while you are here; I promise, it is much easier. You reach the boat launch from an elevator. The boats are bigger and you don't have to lie down. But you should see the underwater nativity," Dom said. "Or perhaps we can go to Baia, where you can see an entire underwater villa. Promise you'll say yes."

"I would be delighted."

"Then we must seal the arrangement with a kiss."

Their lips met gently this time, with a tenderness that made Stephanie shiver. She could not deny her attraction to the handsome man across from her.

Soon, they were back at the docks and boarding the return ferry. The ride back to Sorrento passed in something of a fog for both of them; they spoke little, but sat close together on the ferry. Dom slipped his arm around Stephanie's shoulders; no words were needed.

When they returned to the hotel, Stephanie invited Damiano up for a glass of wine. "There's a small bottle in the mini-fridge; just enough for two."

"That sounds perfect."

They took the elevator up and went into her room. They put their packages on the desk and were quiet for a moment, each gathering their thoughts. For the second time that day, Dom took her in his arms and kissed her deeply.

"I want you to stay," Stephanie murmured. He could feel her heart beat against his chest.

"I would like that very much, *principessa*. But I think tonight we are both too tired to make love."

"What makes you say that?" She sat down on the bed, and he knelt in front of her.

"Because a woman like you deserves to be seduced. To have her shoes removed gently." He unbuckled one of her sandals and slid it off. "To have her feet rubbed and perhaps even kissed. Ovid tells us lovemaking should never be rushed."

He unbuckled her other sandal and sat it next to its mate on the floor, and leaned forward to kiss her again. He unbuttoned his shirt and dropped it over the chair behind him. Then, he gently rubbed each of her feet while she leaned back on the bed.

"That feels so good."

Soon, they were lying next to one another on the bed, entangled as they kissed. The heat of his bare skin through her blouse enflamed Stephanie in a way she never would have expected; his sculpted smoothness invited her caress.

Dom shivered as her lips trailed down his throat to his shoulder and then to his chest. Her tongue caressed first one of his nipples and then the other and he groaned with pleasure.

"I want you." Stephanie's voice was a seductive purr.

"And I want you, *principessa* … but I am willing to wait. Nap now; we will have dinner later and then decide what to do next. There is all the time in the world before we go any further." He kissed her again.

Stephanie snuggled into his arms and was soon asleep with her head on his shoulder. Dom stared at the ceiling and wondered when he had become so bold.

This is not like me at all. And yet, time with her is so short that I don't want to wait.

When Stephanie awoke, covered in a spare blanket from the armoire, Dom was gone. He'd left a note on the dresser:

When I return, we will pour the wine. I will bring dinner.

Stephanie slipped her feet into the beautiful shoes from Capri. She fixed her hair and make-up, and had barely picked up her book when the room phone rang.

"I'm on my way, *principessa.* I hope you like pizza."

Indeed, the pizza Dom brought with him was a delicious and unexpected treat of housemade sausage with broccoli.

"It's from a restaurant down the street that has been in this village for more than one hundred years. It's one of my favorites. I hope you don't mind that we eat it American style, with our hands."

Stephanie's response was to take a slice from the box and bite off the end, closing her eyes in delight as the sweet and sour flavors blended on her tongue.

"If I lived in your village, I would gain so much weight. Everything I've eaten is wonderful."

"If you will excuse my boldness, you would be beautiful in my eyes no matter what, *principessa.*" He opened the mini-fridge and pulled out a split of white wine, which he then poured into two glasses. "To making new acquaintances."

"To new acquaintances. And delicious pizza." Stephanie's laughter was contagious.

Chapter 5

Day 5

Stephanie's head was spinning as Damiano led her to yet a different train platform. They'd started on the little Circumvesuviano, from the station by her hotel. Then, they'd walked to a different train station, one with series of shops that got Stephanie's attention, and caught a subway. Now they were transferring one more time.

"I promise you, *principessa*; you will love this museum. It is worth all the trouble."

When they finally emerged from the train station, they walked up the block to the Naples Archaeological Museum.

"This was the palace of the Bourbon kings," Damiano explained. "They had treasures from Pompeii and Herculaneum brought here for their own pleasure. Archaeology in the eighteenth century was not about learning from the past; it was really more about tomb raiding and showing off the fancy things you found. Smaller artifacts were just ignored or thrown away."

Stephanie could hardly believe her eyes as they went through gallery after gallery of mosaics, frescoes, and other artwork that had literally been cut from the walls of houses in the two towns.

The statues were amazing, but the jewels were the highlight for Stephanie; she snapped numerous photos for her story, and dictated notes into her phone. Damiano was reminded of his days doing research at Berkeley; he'd never considered the kind of details a travel writer might be concerned with.

No wonder she has so many admirers of her work. They must feel as though they are right there with her.

After a quick lunch of *pizza rustico* in a nearby shop, Stephanie and Damiano got back on the series of trains that would return them to Pompeii.

"What did you like best today, *principessa*?"

"Besides your company?" Stephanie pondered for a moment. "I particularly liked the jewelry, but I think my favorite object would have to be the Farnese cup. I've never seen cameo like that before in my life. And to think of how ancient it is; the artisan had a true gift."

Dom contemplated her answer; nearly everyone else he'd taken to the museum had marveled at the huge statues, like the Farnese bull, or the Alexander mosaic. Stephanie's choice, and her emphasis on the unknown maker's talent, warmed his heart. He slipped an arm around her shoulders, drew her close, and feathered a kiss across her forehead.

He later wondered whether that was the moment he started to fall in love with the American journalist.

"May I ask you something, Dom?"

"I have no secrets. Go ahead."

"I know it's none of my business, but why did you come back here after you finished your doctorate at Berkeley? There must have been dozens of choices for you."

Dom looked off into the distance for a moment. "There is something magical about my little village, *principessa.* Maybe it's because my *nonna* lived there when I was a boy; I spent summers with her, visiting my aunt, uncle and cousins as well. It was an escape for a scrawny, bookish boy.

"There were no bigger boys to bully me for not excelling at football, or for preferring to read old myths to super hero comic books.

"As I grew older, it got worse. I only really felt at home in Pompei. I would pretend to myself that I was a gladiator, so that I would know what to say to women. No, it's true. I've never been a bold person, even when I wanted to be. Honestly, once I had that diploma, all I could think of was coming home, and finding a teaching position that would allow me to be stay here forever."

Stephanie studied the handsome, muscular man seated across from her.

You never know what insecurities live inside another person.

"I see how you're looking at me, *principessa*. It doesn't matter how often I go to the gymnasium, or the swimming pool. I can see the changes in my body, and I see that women notice me now. But what has never changed, what will never change, is that inside me still lives that scared little boy who fears he will never be understood."

After a moment, she spoke. "I envy you, Dom. I've never had that feeling of being centered in just one place. I lived all over the

West Coast before settling in San Francisco, and now I have a job that will take me all over the world.

"But here is the thing; I also have reasons to believe that no one will ever really understand me. Now isn't the time to talk about them. But they are there. Perhaps we are not so different after all."

They got off the train to walk to the Circumvesuviana track, and Stephanie found her attention drawn once again to the clothing stores.

"Can we take a few minutes to look, Dom?"

"If we miss the train, another will be along; it is not the last one of the day for a while. Of course we can look."

Stephanie had noticed how differently the local folk dressed from what she was used to at home. She wanted to take a bit of that home with her, but didn't know what she was looking for.

Then, she saw it: a creamy brown v-neck pullover that looked as soft as a cloud. The material lived up to that promise; this was a sweater that could be dressed up or down. Stephanie knew she had to have it.

"I could wear this with jeans or a pencil skirt," she said to Dom. "It's beautiful."

"Then you should get it."

No further encouragement was needed, and Dom insisted on carrying the shopping bag for her.

CHAPTER 6

DAY 7

On the day that Stephanie wanted to visit Herculaneum, Damiano was not available to accompany her.

"My *nonna* prefers her doctor in Naples, and she has an appointment. I will call a colleague and have her meet you."

He wrote out the information on which train stop to take, and suggested she get a taxi to the site. "It is a lot of walking, even though it is smaller than Pompeii. Most of it is uphill; you will want to save your energy for the site itself."

So it was that Stephanie connected with Daniela for a private tour. They walked all over the former resort town, with Daniela pointing out the various sites. The biggest difference between the two sites was the amount of woodwork preserved at Herculaneum; the pyroclastic flow that killed the inhabitants, including many whose skeletal remains were found in former boathouses, had carbonized the wood rather than burning it. Balconies and even a sliding screen were still preserved.

There were two establishments nearby that Daniela described as *thermopolia*, the "fast food" stands of the day. Stephanie had seen similar facilities at Pompeii during her visit, but had only guidebooks to help her know what he was seeing. Having Daniela with her made all the difference.

"No one knows who owned them, really," Daniela was saying.

"Drusus Gaius," Stephanie whispered, wondering how she might have known such a thing.

"Perhaps someone of that name, certainly."

"I must have read it in a guidebook." It was the only explanation that made sense.

They concluded their visit with a walk through the Villa of the Deer, and then the two parted company. Daniela refused the gratuity Stephanie offered. "Damià and I are old friends, and he paid me well for my time. It was my honor to meet you and to share this beautiful place with you."

Stephanie decided to walk back through Herculaneum to the Circumvesuviana station. It was slightly uphill, but she had been so astonished by the city sitting right on the edge of the archaeological site that she wanted to see a little more.

Along the way, she stopped at a greengrocer and bought some of the red-fleshed oranges that he offered by way of a sample. They would be perfect for breakfast in the morning.

CHAPTER 7

DAY 8

"There are so many things I didn't get to see during my first visit to Pompeii and, frankly, without a guide I feel like I missed out."

Stephanie and Dom were in his cousin's restaurant again, sharing an ice cream Napoleon after dinner.

"I can take you the day after tomorrow, if you would like," Dom replied. "Let me know the places you would like to see the most and I will do my best to make sure you get there."

Stephanie handed him her guide map, a few buildings marked.

"Yes," Dom said. "We can do this easily."

Chapter 8

Day 10

Pompeii Archaeological Park

Later

The sun beat mercilessly on the open space where Stephanie lay, the black and tan dog panting at her side.

When Damiano returned to the *quadriporticus*, he had a medic from the archaeology team in tow, along with several fit, young university students. They'd brought a stretcher and enough people to carry Stephanie safely to the gate where they would meet the ambulance. The dog stood up, lowered his head, and bared his teeth; he didn't want to let them near Stephanie. It took one of the students talking softly to the dog and luring him off to the side for them to move the young woman to the stretcher. The dog padded along behind the group, watching as the medics transferred Stephanie to a gurney in the back of their little vehicle and drove off with sirens blaring after telling Damiano which hospital they would use.

The dog then followed Damiano through the site and out the amphitheater gate; they parted company at the *Via Bartolo Lungo*.

The dog went in search of food while Damiano made his way to the lobby of the Hotel Palma to talk with his student.

"*Signorina Giusti*, I need your help. *Signorina Marlowe* has fallen ill and been taken to the hospital in Naples. I need to get some things for her."

The receptionist put down her book and grabbed the appropriate key from the array in front of her. They took the elevator together, and Damiano wasted no time finding a nightshirt printed with cartoon characters, toothbrush and other items that Stephanie might need if she had to stay in the hospital for a while. He put them in the roll-aboard bag he found under the desk. Catching sight of a paperback novel on the nightstand, he put that in as well. He only hoped she'd need it, that whatever had happened was nothing serious.

The young woman also gave Dom a copy of Stephanie's emergency contact information.

After a quick "*grazie*," he walked the short way home, tossed the bag into the passenger seat of his car, and made his way to Naples with the phone on speaker so that he could talk to Raylene. He cursed every one of the twenty-nine kilometers that took him just to the edge of town, and then every driver between him and the university hospital where Stephanie was taken. He had no idea what had come over her, but he knew he needed to be there for the American woman who had captured his attention, and perhaps even his heart.

"*Signorina* Boudreaux, I am sorry to ring in the middle of the night like this. However, *Signorina* Marlowe is on her way to the hospital and I wanted to let you know."

As he drove, Damiano listened to Raylene pour out things he'd never known about Stephanie, like the bout of agoraphobia that overcame her during the second lockdown. She had been frightened of coming to Pompei, but agreed for the sake of her career. There were days when she'd been so upset that even going to the grocery store was too much.

"I had to go places with her or she wouldn't have left the house. But she needed to get back to her work and see the world again, and so she took this job. Whatever happens, you need to make sure she isn't afraid to go out again."

Damiano thought he had never heard anything so brave.

"You let her know that I'm praying," Raylene finished. "I'm glad she has someone there."

At the hospital, the doctors wasted no time. Damiano gave them the bag with Stephanie's personal belongings and they pulled a curtain around the bed while they changed her into the nightshirt. They hooked her up to an IV before opening the curtain and letting Dom pull up a chair next to the bed.

"She'd overheated and dehydrated," the doctor explained. "We will get her temperature down and get some fluids into her. Could you fill out the paperwork?"

Dom completed some forms on a clipboard and then took a seat. He stroked Stephanie's hair, watching the strands of bronze and honey slide over his fingers.

Stephanie was making sounds, talking quietly in her sleep. Dom leaned forward, hearing her speak again in Latin.

“I wish I could see what you’re seeing,” he whispered. He brushed his lips across her forehead and sat back down. He pulled the book out of Stephanie’s bag and opened it to the first page. “I don’t know if this is where you are in the story, *principessa*, but this is where I will begin.”

Dom read the political thriller aloud to Stephanie in a quiet voice that he hoped would not disturb other patients in the emergency department. Keeping his mind on the story kept him from panicking about Stephanie. He hoped the doctors were right, and that she was merely suffering from heat exhaustion. Anything worse simply didn’t bear thinking about.

Beside him, Stephanie dreamed.

Chapter 9
Londinium
61 CE

Suetonius stood in a line of children; he was one of the taller boys, standing out not only for his height but his unwavering green gaze. The serious Iceni boy with unruly black hair had left more than one potential buyer uncomfortable enough to select a more docile-looking child.

"Never let anyone see your fears," his father Claudius had told him.

Well, Pater, I just hope no one can see my knees knocking.

So, he stared staunchly ahead and looked every passerby in the eye until they dropped their gaze. Then the man in a costly tunic came by, walking up and down the row. He examined all of the children, occasionally asking to see their teeth or grasping an upper arm to see how firm it was. Suetonius felt like a horse at market, but kept his peace.

Finally, the man walked over to the slaver and jerked his thumb toward Suetonius.

"He's a likely boy; I'll take him. Name your price." Valerius, the *lanista*, handed over the requested coins to the slaver.

"He's all yours, and may he bring you much wealth." The two men gripped each other's arms above the wrist, kissing one another's cheek to seal the deal. The slaver handed a scroll to Valerius: the receipt that named Suetonius as his property.

"Come along with me, lad."

Valerius led the sullen boy to a waiting barber, where his thick, black hair was shorn close to his scalp. "No lice allowed in my encampment," was all the explanation Valerius gave. "Don't worry, it'll grow back."

Suetonius stared at the *lanista*, but remained silent. When Valerius gestured for him to follow, he did. The humiliation of being enslaved was greater than he'd imagined possible. First he'd been prodded like a horse, and now he'd been shorn like a lamb. He rubbed a hand over his nearly-bare scalp.

"What's your name and age," Valerius asked his new property as they walked along.

"Suetonius." The boy's green eyes flashed as he looked up at his new master. "I have eleven summers."

"You know how to do hard work?"

"I am not one of the lazy Trinovantes who let the Romans into our country. I am of the Iceni."

"You have a Latin name," Valerius observed. He'd let the comment on Romans go for the time being.

"My father was a legionary. The *primum pilus*. He is dead now."

Indeed, his father probably was a legionary, first spear or not. And left his mother, who is definitely dead. Not that it matters now.

"I will train you to be a gladiator. Should you live long enough to fight, you will be called Britannicus. Forget your old name." Valerius reached into a tall basket and handed three blue tunics to the boy."Go to the baths and clean yourself. Put one of these on afterward; the others are extra. Burn the clothes you're wearing now. The *magister* will show you the way."

With a wave of Valerius' hand, Suetonius was dismissed and put under the charge of a man called Rufio. The *magister ludi*, master of the school and also its physician, Rufio was used to seeing miserable young boys brought into the *ludus*. He was not unkind, but neither was he easy on his charges.

Suetonius took an extra long time in the bath, since no one there would suspect the water on his face of being tears. He was nearly grown to manhood, after all; crying was for children. His father had told him that, too. Once he was clean, he put on one of the blue tunics and wrapped the others into a bundle. He held them close to his chest, as though they were a treasure.

Perhaps they are; they're all I have.

Suetonius had dreamed of a future as a tutor; he read books whenever he had the chance. No stranger to hard work, he was also physically fit. It seemed that everyone admired the gladiators, but it was not an ambition he'd held. Still, he'd always been taller and faster than his peers. At least he would not go hungry. But he would never forget his true name.

On the boat back to Rome, Suetonius met the boys who would eventually be his friends and competitors: Hannibal, who was taken from Carthage; Spartacus, from Thrace; and Leonidas, from Sparta. They had already learned not to use their given names; Valerius did not spare the rod. Suetonius had yet to learn that lesson, but he did soon enough.

The food on-board was plentiful if uninspiring, consisting almost entirely of barley gruel. Suetonius wished for a piece of fowl or rabbit, but ate his share without rancor. At least they were not going hungry during their weeks at sea.

The boat brought them up the Tiber and they debarked in a city that looked like nothing Suetonius had seen in Britannia. His village had been modest; this was a big city.

Maybe even bigger than Londinium. Not that I've ever been anywhere but the slave market there. I will keep my eyes open and learn as much as I can.

Valerius and Rufio did a headcount before lashing all of the boys together with ropes around their waists. They were forced to walk single-file, and were not permitted to talk to one another. Valerius was at the front of the line; Rufio brought up the rear.

They walked through the Forum, past its many temples, and through the marketplace. People stared at them and whispered. Suetonius was mortified. A little girl offered him a shy smile; her blue eyes and brown hair reminded him of home. One seldom saw dark hair and light eyes outside of his people. He managed a sad smile of his own as she tugged on her mother's hand and spoke urgently. The woman looked over, shaking her head. He wondered what was said, but put the thought from his mind. There was no point in wasting time on the matter; his fate was sealed.

Eventually, they came to a series of buildings. There, they were brought into the courtyard of what would become their home: the *ludus*. Here they would live, study, work, and train.

The boys were again lined up by height, just as they had been in their respective slave markets. Suetonius thought it foolish; who knew how tall or strong they might be in adulthood? Still, Valerius and Rufio knew what they were about. They walked the line, examining the boys and whispering to one another.

They stopped in front of Suetonius, and it took very little time to make their decision. "This one will be a Thracian," Valerius pronounced. Rufio stated his concurrence and made a note in his wax tablet before they moved on to the next youth.

After making these assignments, which Suetonius could only presume would be explained later, the boys were taken to the barracks. For now, there were eight of them sharing a room, with a cot for sleeping and a small box for their belongings underneath it.

"Keep one clean tunic with you. Put the others in the box. We will go to the bathhouse and the barber now. Afterward, you will eat."

Dirty clothes left in baskets, hair shorn again, baths taken, clean clothes donned. All eight of the boys in Suetonius' cohort stood outside rubbing their heads, waiting for Rufio to take them to the dining room.

As they entered, each boy was given a wooden bowl and horn spoon. The cook slave put barley gruel into the bowl as they walked along the line. At the end, they were given a glass of heavily-watered wine.

"Welcome to Rome, gladiators," Valerius said as they were all seated. "May the gods smile upon us and bring us good fortune, both in and out of the ring."

Suetonius looked around; the men around him ranged from his age to adulthood; all but the newest batch of youths were scarred and muscular, some of them looking nearly prosperous with their heavy bellies. He wondered how he was going to survive.

CHAPTER 10

POMPEII

63 CE

"Julia, I thank you for agreeing to be guardian to my daughter while I seek opportunity in Herculaneum. You won't regret it." Drusus Gaius practically tugged his greying forelock. His thickset body was clad in a wrinkled saffron tunic and blue *pallium*. "Your kindness after my wife's death was a boon to us both."

The woman all the town called Julia Felix, or "Lucky Julia," hoped she wasn't making a mistake. "My daughter Claudia is fond of Drusilla, so they will be companions. I must say, I am confused about why you are not taking her with you. That is, of course, your affair. I warn you, though; should you fail to send the promised funds for her upkeep, I will consider her indentured until your return."

"As you say, Julia. If Drusilla were a son, I could have her help with the business. A girl would only be in the way. Now, I must go meet with Stephanus; the fuller is going to help me set up a tavern in Herculaneum, as I mentioned. May the gods smile upon my small eatery. I will visit every month-end or so with the coins for

Drusilla's upkeep. I know you will ensure that she is well brought up until I am able to take her back."

For her part, Drusilla stood off to the side, holding her puppy. Her father had given her the black-and-tan dog as a gift for her sixth birthday just a few weeks ago. She couldn't believe he was going away, or that he was leaving her behind. She'd promised to be good and not get in the way, but Drusus hadn't listened.

Now she would be alone; her mother, Servilia, had died in the earthquake the year before, when their house was destroyed. After that, they'd rented a room in Julia Felix's large townhouse, with its attached shops and restaurants, private baths, and other fine facilities for people of quality. At least, that was what the sign on the outside of the *praedia* read; Drusilla didn't know what "people of quality" meant.

"Indeed, Drusus, I wish you every success. Drusilla can share Claudia's room for now," Julia said. "Safe travels to you both."

Drusilla was on the verge of tears, her lower lip trembling as she cuddled the little dog even closer. Drusus couldn't help noticing, even as he had hoped for a more stoic departure.

"Don't worry, daughter. Your good uncle, for so you must call him, and I will be back before you know it. Be a good girl, and mind Julia Felix."

"Why can't I go with you? Why can't we go to Rome, like we did before, when Mama was still alive? Why do I have to stay?"

"Things are different now, Drusilla. You need to stay here."

With that, Drusus and Stephanus set out on their journey to the wealthy resort town on the coast. The donkey cart with Drusus' belongings creaked as it rolled over the cobblestones.

"Come on, Drusilla," Claudia said. "I'll show you our room. What's your puppy's name?"

"Invictus."

"Invictus can sleep with us, too. You can come with me to lessons. We're going to have so much fun." Claudia flipped her blond hair over her shoulder with one hand and slipped the other arm around Drusilla's waist.

Julia watched as the two girls walked away together, chattering. She hoped that they could remain friends and equals; she wasn't sure that she trusted Drusus to keep his word. He had always been a little too fond of the main chance, and wouldn't hesitate to put his own needs and desires ahead of anyone else's.

The road to Herculaneum wasn't long; with a cart full of Drusus' belongings, it would take about seven hours to get there. The two men hoped they were not waylaid by bandits, although it was unlikely to happen in broad daylight. There was safety in numbers all the same.

"How different life is now," Stephanus looked around at the countryside. "To think that, just a few years ago, I was buying my freedom and my business. All of those years being paid to pick up people's nightsoil in town, and look at me! I'm able to help an old friend set up his new business with both my time and my treasure."

Drusus nodded. "I can only imagine."

"No, I don't think you can, my friend. You were never a slave. You never had to say 'yes' to things that made you want to choke. You never had to stand knee-deep in piss to clean clothes. The day my former master gave me the nightsoil route was the day my life changed. Everyone in town had to pay me to pick up their chamber pots to collect the urine, and my master let me keep the money. Now I'm a free man with slaves of my own. I don't have to obey orders anymore, and no one can deny me my wishes."

Drusus' mouth straightened into a grim line. "Life is not so simple, my friend. I think we both know that. There is always someone above us to direct things. For instance, you must obey the *aedile*, or a senator."

"Yes, yes," Stephanus waved his hand. "But in daily life? No one may gainsay me. I only wish my Vorena had lived to see this day."

Drusus shook his head. "She was a good woman."

"Hmm. Yes. She was a modest, virtuous person, and she gave me a son. What woman could have wanted more from life?" Stephanus sighed with contentment. "Your Servilia was a good woman as well, although it was a pity she only gave you a daughter."

"I agree, old friend. Still, we were both blessed with good women and have fine children to show for it. Not every man is so lucky; the gods have smiled on us. And, when the time is right for us both, we will perhaps marry again."

"So may it be, Drusus. Any woman I marry will have all of the material goods she could desire; there are advantages to being rich, even if I do say so myself."

Drusus shrugged; the fuller's boastfulness was nothing new and easily ignored. As long as the friendship was mutually beneficial, he really didn't care how much Stephanus bragged about his wealth and privilege.

Soon enough, if Fortuna smiles on me, I will have bragging rights of my own.

CHAPTER 11

Claudia was as good as her word. The next morning, she and Drusilla sat in the peristyle garden, at the back of several rows of boys. Iacobus, a retired tutor who lived in the *praedia*, conducted lessons for all of the children who lived there. This he did in lieu of rent, for Julia Felix was then able to offer this additional benefit to her tenants.

Each student had a stylus and wax tablet; today they practiced writing, while on other days the tablets would be used for sums. Iacobus felt each tablet to make sure the letters were properly formed; his vision had always been poor, and he had feared he would be unable to make a living as it worsened with age. Julia Felix had proposed the private school, where he could teach a smaller group and not have to shout over the noises of the forum. Those noises included other tutors and their students, to say nothing of all the other distractions. Iacobus had accepted her offer, which came with a modest room of his own.

"Drusilla Gaia," he said, after feeling the wax tablet. "You are a new student."

"Yes, Claudia brought me. I have a puppy, but he did not come today."

Iacobus smiled. "Perhaps it is as well. We must focus on our studies when we are in the classroom."

"But this is just a garden."

Iacobus could not help but laugh. "You remind me so much of my late wife. Her name was Flavia. We were never blessed with children; perhaps this is why I took to teaching. One of the things you will learn, Drusilla, is that words can have many meanings. To be sure, this is a garden. But it is also our classroom on pleasant days, just as one of the dining rooms will serve on days when the weather is less in our favor."

Shortly after that, Iacobus dismissed his students for the day.

Claudia and Drusilla went back to their shared room, where Invictus waited patiently for the girls. They took the puppy out to the peristyle, now empty of Iacobus' pupils, and threw a small ball for him to retrieve while also trying to keep him from jumping into the canal where fish were raised for household consumption.

Finally, the dog flopped down on the grass, gnawing on his toy, and the girls sat down on a nearby bench.

"When I grow up, I want to marry Nicia," Claudia announced. "He's the handsomest boy in our classroom. I like his yellow hair and brown eyes. We will live in a villa, with views of the sea. Or maybe I will marry Vorenus; he's not as handsome as Nicia, but his father is the fuller and has a lot of money."

"I don't want to marry anyone," Drusilla replied. "I want to live with my dog and many books. There will be no room for a boy in my house. Just enough rooms for Invictus, me, and our library."

"You will need slaves." Claudia was clear on this point. "Who will cook and clean for you, and do your hair?"

“I would rather look after myself. I can buy food in the forum, and comb my own hair.”

Claudia took her turn throwing the ball. “That would be nice, too. Would there be room for me to visit you?”

“There will always be room for you, Claudia. You’re my best friend, and always will be. Even if you marry Nicia.”

“Haven’t you thought about who you’d like to marry, though? We’re supposed to be wives. Who is the handsomest boy you’ve ever seen?”

Drusilla remembered a pair of green eyes under shorn black hair, long ago in the Roman Forum. “No one you know. Let’s go play with Invictus some more.”

CHAPTER 12

Not all of Drusilla's days were spent in Iacobus' classroom. There were days during which the girls were excused, in order to work on spinning flax or wool for weaving. Every girl was expected to weave a dress length of white wool to be used for her *tunica recta,* the formal wedding gown. The dress was made from a single piece of fabric, belted at the waist with a knotted silk cord.

Drusilla hated spinning; it seemed like her thread unwound every time she tried to add new fibers. Under Julia Felix' patient tutelage, she eventually learned to manage the thread and soon had an entire spool to put on the loom.

The first projects were small: a wrap, or a blanket for Invictus. While Drusilla never learned to enjoy weaving and spinning, particularly because it kept her from the classroom, she developed the skill quickly.

In between times, Claudia showed Drusilla how to pick the locks of the cook's cabinet; there were sweets to be taken. Using two hair bodkins, Claudia could spring the mechanism readily. That the cook would have just given them the treats they took was irrelevant; the point was the game. The cook, who was well aware of what the girls were up to, indulged them by leaving sweets where they could easily be found.

Still, it was in reading and writing that Drusilla excelled. She was first in the exams that both boys and girls took, and prided herself on being able to read well. Iacobus soon started tutoring her in Greek. He also taught her to play draughts, and she proved an apt pupil in the game.

"Your future husband will be proud of your erudition," Iacobus told her one afternoon after she bested him again. "You must ensure that your father negotiates only with learned men. An illiterate man might try to stop you from reading or learning, or even playing at draughts, and that would be a sorrow and a pity."

"Maybe I should marry you when I grow up, Iacobus." Drusilla put the markers in a bag and rolled it up inside the leather playing board.

"My dear girl, I am far too old for you and my eyes are bad. You will find a handsome young man when the time is right, and your father will make all of the appropriate arrangements."

"But I could read to you, Iacobus. I could be your eyes. It would be a good life for both of us. We could play draughts in the evenings after supper." Drusilla didn't bother pointing out that her father had no idea what kind of a man would be best for her; he would assume that wealth was the only thing that mattered. Drusilla loved her father, but had no delusions about his greed.

"My child, your kindness is greatly appreciated. Now, go and play with your dog. It's time for the boys' lessons, and I fear that their ears are on their backs. Unlike you, they need a more physical encouragement."

Chapter 13

Pompeii

Kalends of July, 64 CE

Stephanus, the fuller, watched as Drusilla walked away with the leather draughts board. His son, Vorenus, stood next to him, humiliated at having lost the match to her after class.

"It's shameful, a girl playing that game," Vorenus opined. "Girls should stick to weaving or cooking, or learning how to be a good hostess."

Stephanus, who had in mind a match between his son and the daughter of his old friend, nodded. "A girl oughtn't be too clever, I think."

Iacobus laughed. "Tell me, Stephanus. Do you think it's more shameful that Drusilla plays at draughts, or that she plays it so well that your son is consistently bested by her?"

"Don't be absurd," the fuller scoffed. "Drusilla Gaia was merely lucky this time."

"On the contrary, old friend. Drusilla is a keen strategist. Vorenus makes simple mistakes for two reasons. The first is hubris, for he believes as you do. No mere girl, he thinks, can beat him. The second is that, as a result, he fails to focus on the problem in front of him. You might wish to speak with him, for it is not only in draughts that he fails to pay attention. I say this to you as both a friend and as the boy's teacher."

"I hope to arrange a marriage between these two children one day, Iacobus. Women in my household know to keep to their place. Vorena, gods keep her, certainly knew better than to best me at a game, or anything else."

"Indeed," the tutor murmured as he walked away, remembering a bright young woman cowed with fear after numerous beatings by her husband. He could only hope that Drusilla escaped the same fate.

Chapter 14

Rome

Kalends of July, 64 CE

"Britannicus! Pay attention!" Valerius shouted. "Perhaps I should sell you as a galley slave!"

Suetonius groaned and picked up the heavy wooden practice blade again. His opponent was an older, taller boy whose name escaped him; the two of them were practicing sword drills with double-weight weapons that Valerius knew would make his fighters faster and stronger when the real matches came. Suetonius had been disarmed repeatedly already. His shoulders burned and his arms felt as though they were separate from his body, so sore were they. His tunic was soaked through with sweat, and it seemed that the only part of him that was not in pain was his wavy black hair. Suetonius wore the heavy armor of a Thracian fighter; his opponent was clad as a *murmillo*. The additional weight of his gear made Suetonius even more tired.

Next to them, Leonidas and Hannibal squared off against older trainers. They fared little better than their friend.

"All of you need to pay attention only to the man in front of you," Valerius continued. "Do not worry about what other men in the arena are doing, or where your friends are, or where you want to put your cock later. Those distractions could kill you, and that will cost me money. Focus on where the problem is, not where it isn't!"

Suetonius and the older boy saluted and began again. This time, Suetonius watched the older boy's face; he discovered that his opponent telegraphed his next move by where he flicked his dark eyes. Soon enough, Suetonius was doing more than just defending himself. He was able to go on the offensive. When Suetonius disarmed his trainer, Valerius nodded approval.

"Go to the bath house, young Britannicus. You've earned it. The rest of you, one more round apiece. And focus!"

Suetonius saluted his opponent and walked out of the wooden practice arena. The bath house was a luxury; Valerius had a patron whose villa housed the gladiator school. He didn't know the man's name, or that of any in the household; as a slave, and one under the color of *infamia* for how he earned his keep to boot, it was not his right. Still, that they were permitted to use a private bath was something for which Suetonius was grateful; having to walk through town to the public baths and wait until the slaves' time was humiliating.

To say nothing of how filthy the water was at the end of the day.

Suetonius stripped out of his armor and left it on a shelf. He stopped by his cell to pick up a clean tunic to wear after he washed. There was a basket outside each cell where dirty laundry was deposited for the fullers to collect every week; his Thracian breech clout would land there as well. Valerius issued each slave a certain number of knee-length tunics, which were to be kept in good repair and laundered regularly. Of course, he also kept accounts; the cost of each tunic was entered into a ledger and would be deducted from the slave's share of any eventual earnings before that slave might see a single *as*.

Suetonius' opponent entered the bath house shortly after he arrived.

"Pass me that oil, will you?" Suetonius obliged as the older boy continued. "You are a quick study, Britannicus. It will serve you well."

"I don't remember your name," Suetonius admitted. "Mine is …"

"Britannicus. It's all I need to know. Valerius has named me Vercingetorix, because I'm from Gaul."

"Why does he do that? I've never understood."

"Because, Britannicus, one day we may have to fight to the death. If we don't know one another's real names, it will be easier." He quickly scraped the oil from his body and tossed the strigil on a nearby shelf. "The hot water is going to feel good, Britannicus. You won't want to dawdle."

Time marched on, and Suetonius grew in strength and skill. Vercingetorix became one of his closest friends and most frequent opponents. They practiced regularly, and also learned by observing the older fighters. There was much to remember; those who forgot did so at their own peril, and not all lived to tell the tale.

Chapter 15

Rome

Ides of April, 68 CE

When Suetonius won his first public bout, he had just reached his eighteenth year. He was astonished when a Roman matron asked to have him sent to her. He had no idea that he had grown into a handsome man, or that he might be the object of desire. He had never been with a woman, but Livia taught him well … including how to use his mouth on a woman in ways that most husbands would not consider. He was an apt pupil.

His reputation in the bedroom grew among the women of Rome just as his reputation in the arena grew among the fighters. Graffiti bearing his name sprung up around the *ludus*, and his fellow fighters both teased and envied him.

"Whose bed will Britannicus warm tonight," someone would always call out in the baths, and inevitably a slave would come from some wealthy matron or widow who wanted to be pleasured by the Iceni gladiator whose accent and body were so appealing.

It was nothing but emptiness to Suetonius, but he did as he was bade. Many of the women gave him gifts of coin, which went into his personal *pecuniam*. He was determined that, one day, he would buy his freedom from Valerius and go home to Britain. Perhaps, then, he could be a tutor as he'd always dreamed.

But for now, there were more bouts to fight, and women to please, and no end in sight to either occupation.

Chapter 16

Rome

Kalends of April, 70 CE

Valerius stood in the center of the practice arena, holding a wooden sword and a red woolen hat in his hands. After announcing that Rufio had decided to retire and return home to Capua, he called Suetonius to join him as the other gladiators looked on.

"It is my honor, Britannicus, to present you with the *rudis* and your freedman's cap. You have brought me much honor," Valerius pronounced.

"And also much money," Suetonius replied, one corner of his mouth lifted in a sardonic smile.

"You speak true. And your *pecuniam* has not suffered in the process either; my records show that you have won more than one hundred bouts. What will you do now?"

"First, I shall stand these good friends a drink at the tavern. Good Falernian white wine for all."

The other men cheered heartily.

"And then, if it should please you," he continued, "I would like to stay as an instructor. I know no other trade but this, since I came to it as a child. With your kind permission, if I might teach and occasionally take a bout myself, it will allow me to decide what I wish to do next."

Without knowing when it had happened, this had become Suetonius' ambition. He could no longer readily recall the landscape of his homeland, or the faces of his childhood friends. Most of them were probably enslaved, anyway. Instead, he had found an unusual kind of family in the *ludus*, among the fighters and household slaves. This, he realized, was truly where he belonged.

"You honor me, Britannicus. With Rufio leaving us, I believe you are well-suited to be the new *magister ludi*. We'll put that big brain of yours to use! Now, take the proofs of your freedom, and let's go get that wine."

The troupe traveled all over the empire, entertaining crowds who demanded quality bouts for their games. Under the tutelage of Suetonius and Valerius, the gladiators achieved levels of fame and fortune that few of them expected. Some bought their freedom and became farmers in parts of the world that they liked, especially if they met a local woman who returned their regard. Others returned to the land of their birth, often finding it greatly changed in the years since their enslavement. Suetonius wished each of them well.

Some chose to stay, even as slaves. Their lives were good, even if dangerous during the brief seasons in which they fought; at least they weren't mining copper or rowing galleys. Plus, fame had its advantages. Suetonius didn't hesitate to avail himself of those opportunities. He told himself that it was his due, but Valerius was well aware that the ostentatious, bold trappings the young Iceni man gave himself were to hide a shyness that he wished no one to know of.

CHAPTER 17

POMPEII

IDES OF MARCH, 78 CE

"Claudia, you are the most beautiful bride I've ever seen." Drusilla stood next to her friend as they waited for Nicia in the atrium of Julia's *praedia*. "I am going to miss you so much."

"Nicia's home isn't that far away; you can walk over and visit any time you like. Are you sure I look all right?"

Claudia's blonde hair was bound up in the complicated *seni crines* style, with six braids coming together to create loops and knots around her head. A crown of flowers rested on top of the coiffure, which was in turn covered with a saffron silk *flammeum* veil so fine that Claudia could see through it. Her white wool tunic was immaculate, and tied at the waist with a white silk cord; the "Gordian knot" would be untied by Nicia during their first night as husband and wife. Claudia was gripping her spindle, full of fine white thread, so tightly that Drusilla feared it would crack.

"I don't know why you're so worried," Drusilla replied, tucking an errant brown curl behind her ear. "You've been in love with Nicia since the classroom; you told me when we were children that you planned to marry him."

Nicia finally entered the atrium, a priest of Venus Pompeiia trailing in his wake. Nicia was attired in a fine blue silk tunic picked out in gold thread, with a chalked white toga draped over his shoulder. His brown hair, darker now than in childhood, was dusted with gold to make it look lighter; his head shimmered in the sunlight. His best friend, Vorenus, attired in stark black relieved only by the scarlet edging of his tunic, brought up the rear; his handsome face was sullen and Drusilla wondered why. Surely this was a time for celebration!

The priest read the marriage contract entered into between the two families, describing Claudia's dowry. The material goods had already been transported to the home she would share with Nicia. Then, Nicia put the traditional iron ring on the third finger of Claudia's left hand, and led her out of her mother's house and down the street toward his own. Fellow Pompeiians came out to cheer them along the way as part of the celebration.

Drusilla watched them go, a wistful expression on her face. Stephanus had more than once intimated that he wanted a match between Drusilla and his son, Vorenus; if she had to marry the saturnine youth she'd just watched head out the door, she feared she would not be a happy bride.

Chapter 18
Pompeii
Ides of December, 78 CE

Stephanus took Vorenus aside after the evening meal.

"My son, it is past time for you to wed. I have in mind a union with Drusus Gaius' daughter. This will combine the wealth of our two families."

"I don't want to marry her. Besides, you have said many times that Drusus still owes you money."

"I would forgive the interest on the original loan in exchange for his tavern in Herculaneum. The income from the food stand and the *fullonica* will keep all three of our households in style." Stephanus looked toward the sky and smiled. "Just think of it. Besides, Drusilla is a comely girl. You would be most fortunate to get sons on her."

"I'm in love with someone else, *Pater,* and that person is already married. If I cannot be with that person, I don't want to be with anyone."

Stephanus recalled his son's sullen appearance at Claudia and Nicia's wedding.

Of course; he was in love with Julia's daughter. How thoughtless of me.

"Well, my son, I am indeed sorry for that. Still, a man must marry, and Drusus' daughter is quite the appropriate match."

"Maybe you should marry her, then." Vorenus stomped out of the room and closed the door to his apartments behind himself.

Maybe I should at that. Vorena's been gone many years. No one would look askance. And I could get many a son on a young woman like Drusilla Gaia. I must make a plan.

CHAPTER 19

POMPEII

THREE DAYS AFTER THE IDES OF DECEMBER, 78 CE

Vorenus presented himself at the Temple of Isis. The sanctuary was a favored religious haunt of both slaves and freedmen; Stephanus himself was known to sacrifice there, while still making sure he was seen at the temples of Jupiter Optimus Maximus, Apollo, and Venus Pompeiia.

Taking a deep breath, Vorenus spoke with the gatekeeper and announced his intent to become a priest.

This will silence all the talk of me marrying.

He presented a dowry of one hundred *sesterces*, stolen from his father's lockbox, and made a vow never to partake of sexual intercourse with a woman. He was then taken into the *sanctum*, where he was told to undress. His clothes were taken and replaced with robes woven from blue linen. He would not be permitted to wear anything else, in memory of the flax flowers of Egypt.

Finally, he was taken before the statue of Osiris. "We show ourselves always in mourning for what was done to our god," the priest intoned. "Are you prepared?"

Vorenus nodded and knelt before the altar. A priest appeared with a razor and bowl, and water from the Nile was poured over Vorenus' head. A third priest took up the razor, shaving Vorenus' head and eyebrows, leaving his face completely smooth. Finally, an X-shape was tattooed on the side of his shaven head. The blood from razor nicks and tattooing was wiped away with a soft cloth.

"You will forever after this time be known as Brother Amun, born again like Osiris. I will show you to your cell," the priest said after making some arcane motions toward the altar. "You will remain in contemplation until our evening meal. This is how we all begin."

As the bald senior priest pulled the hood of his robe over his head, Vorenus did the same. The sensation of fabric touching his scalp was a new one; Vorenus couldn't help wondering what his beloved would think.

The senior priest showed Vorenus to a small room, containing only a bed with a thin pad for a mattress and a woolen blanket folded at the end. "This will be your room. The bell will ring for the evening meal. I will introduce you to your brothers then. You will remember all of our names soon enough, Brother Amun. Welcome to our family."

Chapter 20
Pompeii
Kalends of January, 79 CE

Drusilla and Claudia read the painting on the wall outside their favorite eatery.

"Can you believe it, Drusilla? Games for Bacchanalia and Vulcanalia! Those damned Nucerians kept us from having these entertainments for ten years, by order of the emperor."

Drusilla stroked Invictus, who sat patiently at her heel. The elderly dog was still her constant companion.

"Yes, and the games have been allowed back for just as long now. Anyway, you're a married woman, Claudia. Surely you should not have such enthusiasms now that you and Nicia are wed."

"I was sick to death of Nicia before the marriage, even though I didn't say so, and things have not changed even now. He's a lover of men, and he only married me for appearance's sake. He had the nerve to ask whether I would let my *ornatrix* crop my hair like a boy's! Can you imagine? He said that pretending I was a man might be the only way he could put a baby in my belly."

Drusilla felt sorry for her friend. By the same token, her own father's absence and infrequent visits meant that no suitors were pursuing a contract with her. She had to admit to some jealousy. There had been no more talk of a match with Vorenus, now calling himself Brother Amun, since he pledged himself to Isis; on that note, Drusilla felt only relief.

As though the mere thought of Vorenus had conjured his father, the fuller could be seen hurrying toward the two young women.

"Drusilla! Claudia! How delightful to see you." Stephanus hailed the two young women. "Surely you will let me pay for your repast today. It would be my honor. You must not refuse."

Having been put on the spot, Claudia asked for some snails, and Drusilla some duck stew. Stephanus tossed a few *ases* on the counter for the shopkeeper, who put the food in clay bowls for his customers.

"Let me escort you back to the *praedia*," Stephanus insisted. "We can talk for a while. Claudia, as a married woman, you will chaperone Drusilla and me."

Drusilla cringed and wrapped her dark blue mantle closer around herself. Her father's friend made her skin crawl. His thinning brown hair always needed cutting, and his breath smelled of cheap wine. "As you wish, Uncle."

"Surely you are too old to call me Uncle now. You are a beautiful, grown woman." Stephanus licked his lips in a way that reminded Drusilla of Invictus after he ate. "Tell me, Drusilla, what news of your father? As you know, I stood him some funds many years ago in order to open a tavern in Herculaneum. He writes seldom, and visits even less these days."

"I am given to understand that he is well, and no longer rents an *insula*. He has purchased a small home and is contemplating a second shop. Surely he has told you this as well?"

"Indeed, I suppose it slipped my mind. And when will he next be in Pompeii? I should like to meet with him to discuss certain matters."

"He tells me that he will be in town within the next month or so, but that business keeps him in Herculaneum for the moment." She stopped in front of the *praedia*. "Thank you, Uncle, for seeing me safely home. I must go inside and eat now. Good day to you."

Drusilla turned on her heel and walked into the atrium without looking back. Claudia wished Stephanus a good day and followed her friend.

The wealthy fuller, unaccustomed his wishes being denied, stood outside the door and collected his thoughts.

I must make sure she doesn't think of me as an uncle anymore. It has been many years since I have courted a woman; I need to catch up with the times.

Chapter 21

Pompeii

Kalends of February, 79 CE

The *lanista* and his troupe arrived at the outskirts of Pompeii; they'd ridden all day from Neapolis and were tired. Those in the wagons were exhausted with the bumping and bouncing they'd experienced. Those on horseback were better off, but still saddle-sore.

"We will have a barracks here for the duration of our stay," Valerius reminded them. "We will have shelter, and we will have food. The *aedile* here has arranged everything. We will be paid handsomely for our time, and you will all have opportunities to add to your *pecunia*."

The rumblings among the men were a little louder then; perhaps they'd have opportunities to be bodyguards. Or find patronesses; either way might result in some additional money in a slave's purse, and that money might eventually mean freedom.

Suetonius stroked his bay mare's neck as she stamped her forefoot impatiently. "Easy, Cartimandua. We'll be moving again soon."

At the *lanista*'s signal, the group moved through the gate and into the main road of Pompeii. The townspeople on the raised sidewalks watched them pass. Outside one of the biggest villas stood two young women, one blonde and the other dark-haired. The darker one caught Suetonius' attention; her arresting blue eyes reminded him of the women from his homeland. For a moment, he remembered the little girl in the Roman Forum so many years ago. He couldn't take his eyes off of the young woman, even turning to look over his shoulder as he passed.

I must find out who she is.

Chapter 22
Pompeii
Ides of February, 79 CE

"They have to use the *quadriporticus* for barracks; the old building hasn't been fixed. But we can see them at *cena libera*; my mother is hosting it tonight. Isn't it exciting?" Claudia was almost squealing as she danced around the room.

Drusilla nodded, trying to control her emotions. The one they called Britannicus, the *magister ludi*, had been on her mind ever since the day she and her friend watched the gladiators' parade through town. Britannicus sat a fine bay horse, and rode as though he'd been born in the saddle. His green eyes held her gaze for far longer than they should have; he even looked back at her over his shoulder. And she had kept watching until the parade was far out of sight. Careful inquiries with the household slaves had resulted in Drusilla knowing his name, and that he was a freedman. She knew nothing else of him.

I've only seen eyes that color once before.

Julia's words brought her back. "You might remember, daughter, that you are a married woman. Leaving your husband and coming back here doesn't change that."

"He's cruel and horrible, and I hate him." Claudia stamped her foot, reminding Drusilla of when they were children and Claudia didn't get her way at something.

Julia nodded. "I know. Still, he has the right under law to treat you as he wishes, and even to come in here and drag you home. You have no *pater familias* to gainsay him. I think we should consider ourselves lucky that he's left you alone.

Indeed, Claudia's return in the dead of night, one eye swollen shut and a bruise rising on her jaw, told most of the story. Drusilla decided that, if she were ever to marry, her husband would be kind, with a scholarly bent like Iacobus. If he had a face like the *magister ludi*, it wouldn't hurt. All the same, Nicia was proof that a handsome face could hide an evil temper. One never knew.

Later that day, Drusilla and Claudia donned warm cloaks and walked over to the *palaestra* at the *quadriporticus* to watch the gladiators practice. It was bold and probably inappropriate, as Claudia's slave reminded her several times.

"Hush, Felix. Drusilla and I aren't doing anything that other Roman women haven't done."

"Not yet," Felix muttered as he sat behind them.

"Drusilla, who do you suppose that man in Thracian arms might be? Look at those muscles; he doesn't look like the rest of the barley-boys." Claudia winked at her friend.

"There's only one man I'm hoping to see … and with all of them in armor, I can't tell which one he is."

Suetonius could hardly believe his luck. That beautiful, blue-eyed girl from the villa was sitting in the *quadriporticus*. He finished the bout with his student, took off his Thracian helmet, and nodded to her. The smile she gave him was modest without being discouraging, so he walked over. His skin, bronzed from long hours in the sun, glistened with perspiration from his exertions despite the chill in the air.

Don't let her see that you're nervous.

"*Domina*, I crave an introduction. I hope you will excuse my boldness. Here I am called Britannicus; perhaps one day I will share my true name with you. I am the *magister ludi*."

"Bold indeed," Claudia responded. "This is my friend, Drusilla Gaia. I am Claudia Felicia Nicia. My mother is hosting the *cena libera* at our *praedia* tonight; I hope that we might see you there, Britannicus?"

"I would not dare to miss it," he replied, his eyes locked on Drusilla's. "It will be an honor to be received by you."

Drusilla's entire body felt flushed as he spoke. She had never been so drawn to a man in her life. She was past the age when many young women were already married, but her father had been absent for so long that there was no one to negotiate on her behalf. So, she'd made up her mind to choose for herself.

"I shall look forward to seeing you this evening, Britannicus. There will be several *triclinia* arranged as well as seating in the restaurant for the slaves."

"And where might I find you at supper time, Drusilla?"

"I will be at one of the *triclinia*, as will Claudia. Julia Felix has asked us to dine among the free men."

If Suetonius noticed that Nicia went unmentioned in the seating arrangements, he did not remark upon it.

"I hope that you will permit me to dine with you, then. I am a free man, with the *rudis* to prove it. Say yes, and I will count the hours."

"Yes," Drusilla whispered, held in thrall by that green gaze.

"Until tonight, then." Suetonius sketched a bow and walked toward the baths without a backward glance. He did, however, reach down to pet the little black and orange cat who tagged along beside him, her tail straight in the air. She lived in the *quadriporticus*, keeping it free of mice, and was a great favorite among the gladiators; they had named her Penelope.

"Drusilla …" Claudia drew out her friend's name as though issuing a warning, then rolled her eyes and sighed. "I will make sure Mother seats you together."

"You provided the introduction, Claudia. You can hardly pretend to be scandalized now."

"He's handsome, and bold as can be. Have a care, my friend. This worldly man may break your heart."

"He'll probably forget all about me; one of those wealthy matrons coming to gawk at the gladiators will catch his eye and he'll be too well-occupied to bother with the daughter of a tavern owner." Her blue eyes twinkled. "But he certainly is the most handsome man I've ever seen. And look how gentle he was with that cat."

Felix stood and cleared his throat. "If you are to be ready for this evening's festivities, we need to return to the *praedia.*"

Claudia linked her arm through Drusilla's as they walked home. "I have just the dress for you, my friend."

Chapter 23

The atmosphere in the baths was raucous as the gladiators prepared for the evening's entertainment.

"I wonder how many of Pompeii's fine ladies will ask to have their beds warmed tonight," the man they called Hannibal mused.

"Don't worry, Hannibal. Your Carthaginian arse won't be left behind," Spartacus replied. He was Thracian, named after the famous gladiator slave.

Suetonius remained silent, smiling at his friends' jests.

"You're all wrong," Leonidas rejoined. "As usual, *Magister* Britannicus's fucking green eyes and poetic tongue are going to get the ladies' attention first. The rest of us will have to pick up whatever he leaves behind."

"I don't think it's poetry they want from his tongue," Vercengetorix said, making a lascivious lapping gesture between two of his fingers.

"Calm down, my friends. I have eyes for only one woman tonight, and have been invited to dine at her table. I will leave the rest of the fawning matrons to you." Suetonius stood up from the *caldarium* and headed toward the cold plunge, leaving his friends in silent astonishment.

"Britannicus, smitten? That we should live to see the day." Hannibal threw back his head and laughed before sinking back under the hot water.

Chapter 24

The *praedia* was brightly lit to welcome Julia Felix's guests. There were even lamps in the atrium garden, and along the canal where the fish swam. The restaurant was open for seating, and the winter *triclinia* were dressed in their finest drapery.

Claudia and Drusilla had spent several hours with the *ornatrix*, and emerged with hair dressed in curls that spilled over their shoulders, powdered malachite shading their eyelids a rich green, and kohl pressed along their lash lines. Each girl wore a silken tunic with elaborate cords tied to show off her shape; Claudia's was blue and Drusilla's a deep, wine red. As befitted a married woman, estranged from her husband or not, Claudia also wore a dark green *palla*.

The slave at the entryway had a list of the invitees; Nicia's name was notably absent, and Julia Felix could only hope that he would have the good sense to stay away. Valerius had promised her that the members of his troupe would not hesitate to serve as security should she say the word. That she would discuss this delicate family matter with the *lanista* showed the depth of her worry, regardless of what she'd told her daughter. As far as Julia was concerned, Nicia should have been fed to a pool of lamprey eels for what he'd done to Claudia.

The weather threatened rain, as happened so often at this time of year. The hypocaust that heated the baths also kept the floor warm and would make their guests comfortable.

When the gladiators came in with their *lanista*, the simply-clad slaves made for the restaurant. All were enthusiastic over the treats to come; the *cena libera*, after all, could be their last meal. Suetonius alone among the freedmen wore a *pallium* of finely woven gold wool; he carried himself as though it were a chalked toga over his shoulder. His tunic was deep green silk of a rough weave, the neck and hem bound in gold ribbon of a similar hue to the *pallium*. At his waist, the *rudis* hung from a leather belt. Heavy gold bracelets encircled his wrists; everything about him exuded power. He bowed over Drusilla's hand and sketched a kiss across her knuckles.

"You honor me with your invitation, *domina*."

"We will dine in the Venus *triclinium* tonight. Please, follow me." She turned, looked over her shoulder coquettishly, and walked toward the back of the house.

The *triclinium* was painted in the latest style, with a mural of Venus Pompeiia arising from the sea. Platters of dainties, cut into bite-sized morsels, were arranged on a table in the midst of three couches. Long forks allowed the diners to reach the bits they wanted for their own plates; they ate with their fingers.

Slaves, many of them rented for the evening, removed the shoes of each diner and washed their feet in warm, perfumed water before they reclined on the couches for the meal and conversation. Musicians played in a central area, so that they could be heard in the background regardless of where one was seated.

Other slaves passed along the couches with basins of water and towels so that guests could rinse their hands before dining. Suetonius was bold enough to slip his hands into the basin just as Drusilla did and gently touched her fingers.

"Your pardon, *domina*, I did not notice," he said, smiling lazily as he dried his hands and watched Drusilla blush to the roots of her hair.

The first course consisted of egg dishes and cut-up fruits. Drusilla made small talk with all of the diners, as etiquette dictated. Then, when the second course came, she directed her attention to the man sharing her couch.

"You must taste this Parthian chicken," Drusilla picked up a small piece. "It has the flavor of mushrooms, although there are none in the dish. Julia Felix has the most amazing cooks."

Suetonius held her wrist gently and leaned forward, taking the savory morsel from her hand rather than choosing from the plate. He held her fingers in his mouth briefly, swirling his tongue around them.

Drusilla's cheeks grew warm.

"Delicious," he said at last.

"You are bold, *magister*."

"Indeed. It is how I won my freedom." He picked up another piece of chicken from the platter and popped it into his mouth. "In any case, the repast is far beyond the fava bean and barley *puls* that the fighters usually eat. Still, I would rather talk about books."

"Oh! I love to read, I have been studying Ovid …"

Suetonius watched her face, so lively as she talked about the book she was reading. He had never met a woman who cared about anything more than household matters and children. He had seduced plenty of them without a second thought. Drusilla Gaia was different from the rest.

He glanced over to see his friend Vercingetorix deep in conversation with the daughter of the house, Claudia. Even during their short time in town, he had heard rumors that Claudia's husband neglected her — in more ways than one — and was physically cruel. Suetonius hoped his friend would exercise due caution, for the flirtation between the two was blatant. More than one gladiator in the *ludus* had been sold away at the behest of an angry husband. Physical cruelty toward one's wife and slaves was no crime, but bedding a married woman could be.

Then came the third course, when sweets were served. The townsfolk now walked through the *praedia*, taking their time to watch the gladiators eat; this was the purpose of the *cena libera*. Wagers would be made based on observations during the evening. Assignations would be requested by ladies of means. The next day, the fighters would hear the sound of the *cornu* and go into their battles. This was a night for celebration.

One man in particular noticed the intimacy between Suetonius and Drusilla. Stephanus, the fuller, glowered at the pair, refusing to admit to himself that he was envious. He could only watch them from a distance; his couch was in an unfavorable position far from the tables due to his late arrival and he had to wait for slaves to bring the trays around after the other guests were sated with each course.

Drusus' daughter had, as he'd observed many times, grown into a beauty, and Stephanus found his lusts stirring as he watched her share a plate with the *magister ludi*. Despite the fashion for small-busted women, Drusilla's corded dress showed off her curves and tiny waist. Stephanus wished he'd worn a circlet of some kind; he pushed at his lank brown hair in an effort to cover the bare spot on the back of his head. Even his freedman's cap would have helped, but he didn't like to call attention to the fact that he'd been a slave.

Well, if he was no longer young, he was at least wealthy. And he didn't make any pretenses with his attire, either. His tunic was of the finest wool money could buy, dark blue with green ribbon binding at the neck and hem: understated and costly. He had never been a handsome man, but a smart father would overlook that when making a match. And not for his son, Vorenus, either; the nerve that boy had, taking the robes of Isis and calling himself Brother Amun. No, Drusilla would be his. Stephanus would not hesitate to draw on his friendship with Drusus Gaius in order to press his suit, and perhaps would lean on forgiving the loan made so many years ago before Drusus went to Herculaneum in exchange for the girl.

Yes, that would do perfectly.

He ignored the fact that Vorenus had put the idea of pursuing Drusilla into his head in the first place; so far as Stephanus was concerned, the plan was all his.

After the meal, Suetonius asked Drusilla to walk in the garden with him. Marcus Lucretius Fronto, who was running for *aedile* and was the evening's master of ceremonies, had announced the evening's discussion subject: why A is the first letter of the alphabet. There were some barely muffled groans as slaves circulated for more hand-washing and to place wreaths of grape leaves on each diner's head.

Drusilla agreed; the two slipped on their sandals and made a discreet exit. Felix followed at a respectful distance, close enough to interfere if necessary but far enough away to afford the two a modicum of privacy.

"You are quite the conversationalist, Drusilla," he said. "I enjoyed your thoughts about Ovid's work. Certainly more interesting than a discussion of why alpha and not omega. This Fronto seems fond of his own voice."

"You honor me, Britannicus. I had an excellent tutor, Iacobus, who has apartments here. Truthfully, I am grateful to have been educated at all, let alone to have a learned man such as yourself consider my opinions about books. If I may speak plainly, I did not expect a gladiator to be a man of letters. When we first met at the *ludus*, I thought you arrogant, but I know better now. I have gained much wisdom this evening in your company. As for Marcus Lucretius Fronto, he is a politician; one can expect nothing else."

"You flatter me, Drusilla. You must call me Suetonius. My true, given name is Marcus Suetonius."

"Suetonius."

The threatened rains began, drops splashing in the canal. Suetonius pulled a loop of his woolen mantle over his arm to shelter Drusilla as the two hurried under cover. Drusilla told him where her apartments were, and he walked her to the door.

"I very much like the way my name sounds when you say it, Drusilla." He held her gaze, much as he'd done earlier. "And your eyes, in the moonlight, are like the lakes of my homeland. Though I have not seen them in many years, I have not forgotten their beauty. I have only seen eyes like yours once before, in the face of a little girl, as I was marched through the Forum in Rome on my way to the *ludus*."

He was the green-eyed boy in Rome. Venus, help me!

"You are too kind." Drusilla dropped her gaze; she had briefly forgotten that Roman women were to be modest.

Suetonius put his hand under her chin and gently tilted her face toward his. "I am no such thing, my princess. I am bold, perhaps a little arrogant, and some say dangerous. I will prove it, if you will let me. Kiss me, Drusilla."

"Suetonius …"

This time his name was a sigh on her lips … lips that he claimed in an embrace more passionate than she'd thought possible. No stolen kisses from the local lads or even a pretty slave boy here and there had made her feel like this. It was the same warmth that flooded her body when he'd raked those green eyes over her at the *palaestra*, and again when he'd taken food from her fingers at dinner. This time, that warmth came from a deeper spot and rose up through her like a flood. She slipped her arms around his neck and kissed him back with an ardor that he had not imagined a well-bred Roman woman to possess.

At length, Suetonius moved his mouth from her lips to her ear, his breath hot as he whispered "I would share your bed if you will have me."

"I have given myself to no man before." The confession should have felt like a point of honor, but instead Drusilla's face was hot with shame and she trembled in Suetonius' muscular arms.

"You are frightened," he murmured, his lips caressing her ear as he spoke. "I will never take by force that which may be offered of your own accord, so you need not fear. I will take my leave this night with my fellows, but perhaps I may call tomorrow and speak with your father."

"My father is at Herculaneum, and I do not know when he will return."

"Then I will call tomorrow and speak to you in the daylight. I will count the hours until then." Suetonius kissed Drusilla again, and left her with her thoughts as she slipped into her apartments and barred the door behind herself.

She was hardly alone, though; in the shadows, Stephanus had seen everything.

Time for me to write to Drusus and let him know about this infamous barley-boy. Once he returns, we will see what is what. And whether he will give me Drusilla's hand.

Alone in her room apartments, Drusilla took an oil lamp from a waiting slave, a new girl whose name she could not remember, and went into her sleeping chamber. She placed the lamp in a wall niche and sat down on the bed.

"Shall I take your hair down and help you prepare for bed, mistress?" The young slave girl's Latin was hesitant as she stood in the doorway.

"Yes, please. But do so quietly. I have things to think about and don't want any idle prattle."

The girl did as she was told.

Chapter 25

Pompeii

Kalends of March, 79 CE

True to his word, Suetonius called on Drusilla in the morning, and on many other occasions thereafter. One of the things they talked about was his home country; even though it had been many years since Suetonius had seen it. He told her of how they slept in furs to keep warm in winter, and about his village. He even told her how the women of his tribe wore their hair, caught at the nape in metal clasps, but with a braid hanging from each temple. Drusilla occasionally wore her hair that way when they met, despite it being considered unfashionable.

On this particular day, Suetonius brought a scroll with him, and read to her from Lucretius' *Third Book of On the Nature of Things* as the two sat side by side on a bench in the peristyle.

"Even at last when the lovers embrace and taste the flower of their years, eagerly they clasp and kiss, and pressing lip on lip breathe deeply; yet all for naught, since they cannot tear off aught thence, nor enter in and pass away, merging the whole body in the other's frame; for at times they seem to strive and struggle to do it. And at length when the gathering desire is sated, then for a while comes a little respite in their furious passion. Then the same madness returns, the old frenzy is back upon them, when they yearn to find out what in truth they desire to attain, nor can they discover what device may conquer their disease; in such deep doubt they waste beneath their secret wound."

Suetonius rolled the book of poems and placed it on the bench next to him. "I fight in two weeks' time. I hope you will be there."

He split a honey pastry in two and gave half to Drusilla.

"You told me that you had retired, and now only taught the other gladiators." She finished her roll and licked her fingers, which distracted Suetonius so much that it took him a moment to reply.

"The patron of our games has asked me to fight, and I cannot refuse."

"Who is the *editor* this time?"

"Stephanus, the fuller. He has sponsored the games in honor of Bacchanalia."

"I shall be there, Suetonius. I will sacrifice to Mars, that you may be victorious." Drusilla's voice raised, and her eyes flashed. "Have a care; my uncle is jealous of you, and I suspect he wants you to be killed. But I won't let that happen. Ever. How I hate him."

Drusilla's father had written to her, saying Stephanus had expressed concern with the company his daughter kept, and hinting that he might wish to court Drusilla himself. The effrontery had shocked Drusilla to her core, and she now went out of her way to avoid her father's friend.

"Now, now. Valerius will not allow a fight to the death. His gladiators are too valuable." He glanced over at her. "If I am victorious, what would you leave on the altar? A lock of your hair? A piece of fruit? A bird from the marketplace?"

"Something I would give willingly to you."

"And what might that be, Drusilla?" He dipped his hand into the canal water next to them, rinsed the remains of his breakfast away, and traced a damp finger along her neck and collar bone as he faced her full-on.

"I think you know."

"Tell me, princess."

She leaned forward and whispered in his ear. "My maidenhood."

"Do not tease me, Drusilla." His breath was hot against her ear, which was exposed by her hairstyle; today her brown locks were swept up in a fillet. The pearls hanging from her lobes swayed as his lips brushed across them.

"Never."

"If you speak true, then I must win the day. For now, let me claim a kiss before leaving. Can you meet me at the theater? The players are performing *Pseudolas*, and I think you will enjoy it. If it please you, we can take a meal afterwards to discuss it. I only wish we could sit together."

Drusilla agreed to attend the play, then gave him a kiss and watched him go. She went to her apartments for a veil before visiting the temple in the Forum. She purchased a bird from the marketplace and went to the altar of Mars, where the priests made the sacrifice on her behalf as she prayed. Even knowing that few gladiatorial fights except those between criminals ended in death, the sport was dangerous; she could only offer her wishes, rising to the heavens on altar smoke.

For Suetonius' part, he returned to his cell and closed the door behind himself. He envisioned Drusilla in the clothing of his tribe's women, unclasping her brown hair so that it lay loose over her shoulders, and lying back on a pile of furs. He imagined holding her hands over her head while they coupled, keeping her there until she cried out with pleasure. He stroked himself until he reached his climax, wiping his body with a tunic bound for the laundry basket. Slaking his needs this way would not stand for much longer; he had to win the bout, and he had to have Drusilla for his own.

As for Stephanus, he spent the morning with a *tonsor*. The Numidian slave, Iosephus, had a reputation for skill, and Stephanus wanted nothing but the best. The two went to Stephanus' garden so that the barber could work in the sunlight.

"I want my hair dyed black, cropped, and curled," he pronounced. If that was the look Drusilla favored, he would adopt it. Everyone knew women were shallow and fickle; surely this would cause her to view him favorably.

"As you wish, *dominus*."

Iosephus opened his case and arranged his tools on a nearby bench. He opened a jar containing a foul-smelling mixture of leaches and vinegar that he smeared all over Stephanus' head and brushed across his brows.

"We will need to leave it this way for a few hours before I pour water through it," the barber explained. "Then I will cut your hair and curl it with a *calamistrum*. You will be as handsome as an emperor."

Flattery was part of a *tonsor*'s stock in trade, to be sure. Still, Iosephus was sometimes glad that his bronze mirrors did not give the most accurate reflections in the world. This was shaping up to be one of those days.

While they waited, Iosephus lit a small brazier so that the coals would be ready to receive and heat the conical *calamistrum*. He also set out shears, a razor, and a preparation of his own making, comprised mostly of lanolin and rosewater, that would keep curls in place once they were arranged.

Another slave came in, this time with tweezers and towels. He set about plucking the sparse greying hair from Stephanus' chest and under his arms. It was painful, but Stephanus had seen how women admired the smooth-muscled barley boys; if modeling his appearance after theirs was what it took to win Drusilla's attention, he was more than willing to endure a little discomfort.

When at last the horrid mess was rinsed from Stephanus' head, Iosephus sat about cropping the black locks.

"I have just this day studied a statue of Emperor Titus," he said. "I will cut your hair short and curl it all over, in the style that our emperor favors. You will be at the height of fashion."

"Most excellent, Iosephus."

One of Stephanus' slaves entered the peristyle where Iosephus was going about his work. He held a bale of snow-white fabric, freshly moved from the fullery's roof where it had been cleaned and pressed.

"I have the wool you requested, *dominus*."

"Excellent. See that it is wrapped in silk. The blue, I think, to match the lady's eyes. No. The Tyrrhenian purple, picked out in gold embroidery. Then, bring the second-best litter to take me to the *praedia* of Julia Felix; I wish to visit Drusilla Gaia and present her with these goods."

Iosephus, standing behind Stephanus as he wrapped the dyed hair around the curling rod, rolled his eyes. Much was now explained.

Stephanus' smile curled up in a smug fashion. *Soon, that barley boy will be dead in the arena. Drusilla Gaia cannot help but notice me now.*

Indeed, Drusilla noticed. She could see his arrival from the peristyle where she had been reading aloud to Claudia after returning from the temple.

He lives three doors down. What a pretentious fool, to have slaves carry him here.

Stephanus stepped down from his litter and told the slave on duty to send for Drusilla. He paced around the atrium, awaiting her arrival.

"Uncle," she said, as she came in from the garden. "I did not expect you on this day." She smoothed the pale, creamy linen of her tunic. "I would have requested food and drink, and put on a nicer dress."

"You look beautiful, Drusilla. I came to make a present of some material to you." He gestured to his slave, who came forward with the bundle. "Silk and fine wool for you, my dear."

"Uncle, you are too kind. It is neither my birthday nor a feast day, so I am sure you will understand my confusion."

"I thought you might make yourself a dress and *stola* from these materials, and wear them to the gladiatorial games I am sponsoring. And perhaps, after the games, you will be my hostess at the banquet I am hosting that evening. I will also be happy to provide jewels if you would like them. Say you will, Drusilla, and then I will speak to your father."

"Uncle …"

"You know I am not your uncle; please stop calling me that."

"Stephanus, I am flattered by your attentions. But you are my father's friend and my father's age …"

"Indeed, but you may have noticed that I am looking much younger this day. I believe you favor men with black hair cut into short waves. Look what I have done for you."

Drusilla had, of course, noticed the flat, unnatural color of Stephanus' hair. "That was not necessary."

"I will do whatever I think necessary to improve my chances in your eyes. And I am sure your father, who still owes me much after so many years, would be more than happy with our match." Stephanus grabbed her hand.

Drusilla's eyes widened and her jaw dropped open. It took her a moment to recover and pull her hand away from the fuller's grasp.

"Then perhaps my father should marry you. Two foolish old widowers together would perhaps keep one another out of trouble."

She turned on her heel. Stephanus sent his slave after her with the fabric and would not depart until she accepted the materials.

On the way out the door, Stephanus took it into his head that the slave was to blame for his poor reception and struck him repeatedly. The poor man's eye was swelling shut when he joined the others to pick up the litter and carry their master home.

As soon as they were gone, Drusilla tried to give the bundle to Julia Felix. "Make something for yourself with this; I have no need use for it."

"These are valuable fabrics," Julia replied. "You should put them away; you never know when they might be of use."

"Yes, but Stephanus forced them on me. I don't want him or his gifts."

Drusilla returned to her apartments and dumped the costly material unceremoniously into a chest. She went back out to the peristyle, where she and Claudia had been talking before Stephanus arrived.

"He gave me dress material in wool and silk," Drusilla announced as she dropped onto the bench next to her friend. "And then he had the audacity to talk of a match between us! As I told your mother, I want neither Stephanus nor his gifts."

"I envy you. When Nicia courted me, he gave me nothing as fine as that. Besides, Stephanus came himself; he might have just sent a slave. He must truly love you."

"If you want the materials, Claudia, they are yours." Drusilla pinched the bridge of her nose. "Stephanus makes my head ache. And I don't think that he loves me at all. He thinks that his wealth can buy anything; I'm no different from a slave, a chair, or a jar of *garum*, so far as he's concerned."

Claudia put her arm around her friend and hugged her. "I will take them in trade for the blue-green silk I bought; the color would suit you well. Let us take the fabrics to my home, and get a swatch of the silk. My woman can make you up a dress, perhaps in the Grecian style. We can go to the marketplace and buy some *fibulae*; the swatch will help us decide which ones look best."

The jeweler's booth was hardly doing any business when the two women entered, followed by Felix with his mistress' shopping basket and money pouch. Drusilla looked at the various pins on offer, but nothing caught her fancy. However, she did see a set of blue beaded earrings and matching necklace that she liked.

"*Faience*, all the way from Egypt, *domina*," the jeweler informed her. "You have an exceptional eye."

"We'll take those," Claudia said. "Please wrap them up."

From across the forum, Suetonius saw Drusilla in the jeweler's booth. He hurried around the marble gate into the *macellum*, catching up just as the group were leaving with their purchases.

"*Ave, domina.*"

"*Ave, Magister.*"

"Felix, I think we should consider a visit to the weaver…" Claudia began.

"Oh yes, *domina*. But the nearer one, you know …"

"Those two are not even subtle," Drusilla said as her friend went down the way to look at woolens that would be out of season soon.

"Hardly." Suetonius smiled. "Still, I am glad for a moment to speak. What brings you to market today?"

Drusilla showed him the swatch of silk. "Claudia's woman is going to make me a dress, but I need pins for the shoulders. I haven't found any that I like yet."

"If you will permit me," Suetonius put his hand on Drusilla's waist and guided her into a different jewelers' booth. "I saw some brooches here just the other day that may suit."

Indeed, the counters were filled with beautifully enameled metalwork, and Drusilla found a pair of brooches that she deemed perfect: golden peacocks with sapphire eyes and elaborately enameled tail feathers.

The jeweler named his price, which Drusilla realized was too dear for her pocketbook. Accepting the beads from Claudia was one thing, but she couldn't ask this of her friend.

Suetonius, for his part, opened his purse and put the requested number of *sesterces* on the counter without batting an eye.

"The peacock, *domina*, is beloved of both Juno and Venus. I can imagine no more appropriate adornment for a woman of your intelligence and beauty. Please accept them as a gift from me."

The jeweler handed Suetonius two leather bags, each containing one of the pins.

"It would be my honor, *Magister*."

Outside the booth, Claudia and Felix watched as Suetonius feathered a kiss across Drusilla's brow before coming to meet them. He put the two pouches in Felix' basket.

"Let me walk with you until you reach home. I would not want the precious cargo, or its owners, to come to any harm."

Claudia and Felix could only smile, and by unspoken agreement walked a few paces behind the young couple so that they could speak in private.

That evening, Drusilla and Felix sat in the highest rows of the theater. She could see Suetonius several rows below her, with the other freedmen. Stephanus was nowhere to be seen; he did not share Drusilla's love of intellectual pursuits.

After the performance was over, Suetonius waited for Drusilla. Felix found an excuse to walk several feet away from the two as they spoke. They walked the short distance to the *quadriporticus*, where Suetonius would sleep in his lonely cell.

"I do not have the words to describe how I feel for you," Drusilla confessed after he kissed her again. "You are awakening things in me that I have never known."

"You are well and truly becoming a woman before my eyes, my princess." He caressed her face gently. "And you make me want to be a better man. I believe that Venus Pompeiia has brought us together, and her son Cupid has nicked us both with his arrow."

He brought his lips to hers once again. "Your slave is waiting to see you safely home, my beloved. We will see each other on the morrow."

Chapter 26

Pompeii

One day after the Ides of March, 79 CE

Bacchanalia

The day of the games dawned warm and clear. Drusilla and Claudia sat in the highest row of the amphitheater, along with all of the other women of Pompeii and their household slaves. The awnings were pulled up to shade the ladies from the unseasonable sun, and food vendors walked through with offerings of wine, water, and snacks. Claudia wore a new dress and *palla* made from the material Drusilla gave her. Drusilla was resplendent in her silk dress, the peacock brooches holding it at the shoulder and a golden cord nipping in the waist. The *faience* beads and earrings completed her ensemble. Her hair was held back from her face with blue enameled combs, a cascade of curls streaming down her back.

The program began first thing in the morning, with some chariot battles and a couple of female gladiators fighting each other. There were no executions that day, so after a lengthy break the musicians, referees, and gladiators came through the gate. Stephanus, in the *editor*'s box, accepted all of the combatant's salutes. Ten pairs were fighting, according to the program, in various styles.

Over all the crowd noise, Drusilla heard the only name she cared about "Britannicus *Librus* versus Vercingetorix."

Drusilla recognized Suetonius by his Thracian armor; they were at the far end of the field from her and it wasn't easy to see him. His opponent was a *murmillo*, another heavyweight gladiator.

Claudia grasped Drusilla's hand. "Surely not. The two are great friends."

"What makes you say that?"

"Because I've been seeing Vercingetorix whenever I get the chance. We talk."

"You and I will talk later," Drusilla responded, then turned her attention back to the arena.

Both men drew blood, but soon the *murmillo* was down and did not get back up again until the referee stopped the bout and Suetonius helped Vercingetorix to his feet. Drusilla saw the *murmillo* lift a finger toward the editor's box; Stephanus took his time but gestured for mercy. Suetonius received the victor's laurel, and helped the other man limp out through the gate.

After the *cornu* signaled the next event, with animals fighting one another, Drusilla excused herself and left the arena. This was the part of the program that her soft heart could not tolerate.

Stephanus came down from the editor's box, and interrupted her as she tried to leave.

"You look very beautiful today, Drusilla. Might I ask why you do not have a new dress, though? I gave you silk and wool."

"On the contrary, Uncle. The dress and jewelry are entirely new. The silk and beads were a gift from my foster sister, Claudia. I gave your material to her in gratitude; as you may know, she has a neglectful husband."

Stephanus took hold of Drusilla's upper arm and squeezed. "Those fabrics were a gift to you."

"Yes, and since they were mine, I did with them as I pleased."

"You have not accepted my invitation to sit at my side during the banquet tonight, either. Why is that?"

"I am feeling indisposed and will not be in attendance. Why do you think I'm leaving the games?"

Stephanus leaned closer and growled into her ear. "Your ingratitude angers me, Drusilla. Remember, your father is in my debt."

"Let go of me, Stephanus. I am not yours to command."

Drusilla yanked her arm away, and turned her back on the gaping Stephanus. She crossed the street and met Suetonius in the *palaestra*. He dropped his helmet and gear on the back of a wagon, collected a cup of foul-looking *posca* mixed with ash, and gestured for Drusilla to follow him. They walked away from the gathered vendors, other gladiators, and prostitutes. They stood next to the swimming pool as Suetonius gulped down the drink; the noise of the water would make it difficult for others to hear their conversation.

"You look beautiful, Drusilla. I am honored that you wore the brooches today." He took her hand and dropped a respectful kiss on her knuckles.

Drusilla shivered at the sensation, then cleared her throat. The time had come for unmaidenly boldness.

"You must come to the *praedia* this afternoon, Suetonius. I have arranged for us to have the baths to ourselves, so that you may bathe and I may dress your wounds in myrrh."

"Drusilla, this is a dangerous game for you to play. There is still time for you to change your mind." Suetonius swiped his arm across his eyes to clear the sweat away.

"I am not playing, Suetonius. I made a promise to the gods, after all. My prayer was answered." She laid her hand on his upper arm. "Besides, I want to do this with you."

"I will be there within the half hour, then. Kiss me, my princess, and let me count the minutes."

Drusilla did as he asked and took the short walk back to the *praedia*. On the way, she bought a small drinking glass commemorating the bout she had just witnessed; the vendor created images of Britannicus L. besting Vercingetorix by adding names to pre-painted images showing a Thracian beating a *murmillo*. She would put it on her altar next to the *lares*, in gratitude for hearing her prayers.

Drusilla had paid Felix to make sure she would have the *praedia*'s bath complex to herself. The massage table was draped with clean coverings, and the various balms and oils organized for ready access. The *frigidarium* and *caldarium* were both clean, and fresh water filled them at appropriate temperatures.

Drusilla changed her silken gown for a pale blue linen tunic that came down to her ankles. On her feet were delicate sandals, decorated with blue stones. She took the combs from her hair so that it fell loose over her shoulders. She paced the floor, wringing her hands as she considered what she'd set in motion. While she had no doubts, she knew that a thing done could not be undone. She'd set her sights on a man who was a former slave, whose profession was universally looked down upon … and somehow none of that mattered.

Felix tapped at the door. "Britannicus has arrived."

He stepped back and the gladiator entered the room. Felix slid the wooden screen shut behind him, and the two were alone.

Suetonius didn't speak; he merely held Drusilla's gaze as he stripped off a wine-red tunic and dropped it on a nearby bench. Every scrape and cut from his bout was displayed on a body that would have inspired a sculptor and, perhaps, stirred envy in the gods.

"I ask you again, Drusilla, are you sure of what you want?"

"More sure than I have been of anything in my lifetime."

She opened a jar of myrrh unguent, rubbing it gently over his his injuries. Suetonius' eyelids fluttered as she stroked his body, the ointment easing his pains.

"Please, lie down here." She indicated the table, as she switched to a bottle of lime-scented oil. Her touch alternated between firmness and feather-light, and now and again she would drop a kiss on some muscle or other.

Next, the *strigil*, scraping off the sweat and any remaining soil. He stood then, proud and tall, as Drusilla continued with her caresses.

"Join me in the tub," he whispered. "I want to see all of you."

Drusilla took off her tunic and undergarments and he helped her into the water. "Sit on the edge," he whispered. It was there that he set his mouth to her plucked, bare sex. Suetonius used his tongue to tickle, tease and stroke, his hands firmly on her bottom so that she didn't slip.

"You are as sweet as honey, Drusilla. Maybe I should call you *Meilichia* ..." He then kissed his way up her abdomen until he reached her breasts, where her nipples received the same treatment.

Then, he brought her up against the marble wall, the coolness of the stone contrasting with the heat of the water and his body. He parted her thighs, and slid his manhood between them, encountering a brief resistance before he was all the way in. Drusilla winced a little.

"Would that this were a Tyrrhenian bed instead of a bath house; you deserve more," he whispered, his breath warm upon her ear. "The pain is brief, princess, but I promise you pleasure afterward."

Suetonius was as good as his word. He kissed her neck and throat, holding her firmly against the wall as he stroked in and out of her wetness. He tangled his fingers in Drusilla's hair, growling his pleasure in her ear.

"I … don't understand what I'm feeling," she groaned. "But I don't want you to stop."

"Ah, my Drusilla Meilichia … " He shuddered as her muscles tightened around him, both of them deep in pleasure.

He helped her back down into the tub. "I fear I will have to use the ointment again for you," she whispered.

"It was worth every moment." He leaned back. "I should write to your father, and proffer myself as a suitor."

"It is not necessary."

"Ah, but it is. I think I have been halfway in love with you since I first saw you."

"I confess, I feel the same way. Still, we barely know one another."

"And yet, you sacrificed your maidenhood to Mars for me. Come, Drusilla. Life is short and cruel. Marry me, before your father gives you to someone else."

"I thought gladiators couldn't marry freeborn women …"

"I'm a free man and the *magister*. I can marry where I please. And it is you who pleases me. Say yes."

"Yes, Marcus, I will." It was the first time she'd used his *praenomen*.

"My Drusilla." He claimed her mouth with his.

Their kiss was interrupted as Claudia came in from the public entrance to the baths; she held the key to the door in her hand. "You must hurry out this way, Britannicus. We are now in a state of emergency."

Suetonius slipped his tunic over his head and tied his sandals.

"What is happening, Claudia?" Drusilla pulled a wrap around herself.

"Your father has returned from Herculaneum, and he is in the *tablinum* with my mother right now. I've told him you're in the bath, but I don't think he'll wait for long."

Suetonius kissed Drusilla again. "I will speak to your father."

"Not yet," Claudia said. "He also has Stephanus the fuller with him, and the two are talking of marriage. Drusilla has to talk to him first and convince him not to accept Stephanus' suit. Then she can tell him she has promised herself to another. You have, haven't you?"

"Yes, Claudia," Drusilla replied. "And thank you."

Suetonius gave a grim nod and walked out the side door, just seconds before the main inside door opened to admit Drusus while Drusilla hurriedly wrapped herself in the sheet she'd set aside for her lover. Felix stood behind him, looking miserable.

"Daughter, you have become lazy to be at the bath so long. Why is that?"

"She is sore from her courses, Drusus. I had her soak in the tub and was going to rub her back with myrrh." Claudia forestalled anything else Drusilla might have said.

"Your friend is kind, daughter. Surely you have slaves for that? Never mind that for now. Dress yourself in your finest, and come to greet your father. I have great news for you."

"As I do for you, Father. Shall we meet in the garden shortly?"

"That will be perfect. Thank you." Drusus turned on his heel as the two young women closed the opened jars and bottles.

When Drusilla had put on a fresh tunic and re-arranged her hair in a simple braid, she met her father in the courtyard. They sat side by side on the same bench where she had kissed Suetonius for the first time, and watched the fish cavort in the canal.

"I am sorry to have missed the games earlier today; I am told that there were several spectacular fights. You were only four years old when Spiculus bested Aptonetus *Librus*. That was something to see. Of course, you were at home with your mother." Drusus smiled at the memory. "But that is not what I wished to speak with you about. I have found a rental house for us here in town, thanks to Stephanus. As you know, he has been a great friend to me since your mother's passing. I will arrange to have your things moved out of the *praedia* in the coming days."

"As you wish, Father. I am glad that Uncle Stephanus has been such a help to you."

Drusus turned to face his daughter. "It cannot have escaped your notice, my daughter, that you have long since passed the age when most girls are married and have children of their own."

"While that is true, Father, I don't think that will be the case for much longer. I am glad to speak with you, for I have a suitor."

"I know; he has written to me."

"How can that be? I have only just this morning accepted Marcus Suetonius' suit."

"Who is this Suetonius of whom you speak? I refer to Stephanus, who waits in the *tablinum* to greet you and receive my blessing on your union."

Drusilla remained silent, which was not the response Drusus expected. Surely a young woman who was about to make such a wealthy marriage would have something to say.

When Drusus looked in his daughter's eyes, there was something different in her expression. It had been many months since he had seen his daughter, but he had seen that expression on her mother's face after he'd deflowered her on their wedding night. This was the face of a woman who had known a man: who knew what it was to be a complete woman at last.

"This Suetonius. Have you lain with him? Perhaps you were taken by force and he seeks to make whole the family's loss?"

"And if I did lay with him, what of it?"

"Defiance, daughter? How unfortunate. I suppose this should be expected; after all, I have not been present to ensure that you were well brought-up and protected. I trusted Julia Felix to look after you better than this." Drusus heaved a sigh. "Well, Stephanus need not know."

"You think I would marry the fuller? His home stinks of piss, and he is ill-mannered. He dyes his hair and looks ridiculous." Drusilla stood up and paced the walkway.

"Who is this Suetonius, anyway? Who are his family? Perhaps we can yet negotiate with them."

"He's a freedman, like Stephanus. He's a gladiator, from Britannia."

"This is not a time to make jests, daughter. And how long have you known him, anyway?"

"I am not jesting, father. Suetonius carries the *rudis*, but still makes his living in the *ludus*; he is his troupe's *magister*. And I have loved him since first I saw him in January. In fact, I have loved him ever since I first saw him in Rome."

"Nonsense. You haven't been to Rome since you were a small girl; you could not possibly have seen him there. But that is not the point. You gave yourself to a gladiator. Tell me why I should not beat you to death for this dishonor." Drusus could not look at his daughter. "This is the foolish behavior of a child, not that of a grown woman."

"You told me many times over the years how much you loved my mother. That you were fortunate to marry for love. Why should I not do the same?"

"Your mother was a good woman, from a good family."

"So you have said, many times. And yet, you were from a lower class than she."

"I did not live under the taint of *infamia,* Drusilla. I was a merchant; her father was one of the *equites*."

"He accepted your suit."

"He did, and provided your mother with a good dowry."

"Which, I am sorry to say, we both know you lost over the years by playing at dice."

"I put a roof over your head," Drusus roared.

"You did. And when it fell during my sixth year, you found us rooms in the *praedia*. But you never did put another roof over our heads. You left me with Julia and went to Herculaneum to seek your fortune. You told her that since I was a girl, I would only be in the way. Do you have any idea the pain you caused me that day? There's no use denying it, Father; I heard you myself."

"Stephanus loaned me money to establish a tavern there. I have been quite successful. I even have a woman there, a widow called Rufina, whom I hope to marry. She is pleased with the idea of having two households to manage."

Drusilla could almost see her father puffing up with pride. "Why did you come back, Father? Was it to ensure that I would never be in your way again?"

"I wanted you settled before I returned to Herculaneum."

"And this settlement, with Stephanus?"

"He wrote to me and offered to forgive my debts in exchange for your hand. He warned me that you were in danger of being ruined by some barley-boy and that he wanted to make an honest woman of you. So, I returned. I didn't want to believe him, but it seems he was correct and I am too late."

Felix came out to the garden.

"I am sorry to interrupt, but Marcus Suetonius begs an audience with Drusus Gaius in the *tablinum*."

Father and daughter stared at one another, both red-faced with frustration. Drusilla broke the silence.

"You could at least do him the courtesy of hearing what he has to say." She turned on her heel and walked into the house, leaving her father staring after her.

Heaving a sigh, and looking toward the sky as if he expected the gods to intervene, Drusus followed his daughter. It would hurt nothing to listen. "Felix, have him wait outside. I have another piece of business to discharge in the *tablinum* first."

Drusus found Stephanus pacing the floor.

"*Salve*, old friend. I trust things have been settled to our mutual satisfaction. Where is your daughter? I rather hoped you would bless our union today." Stephanus' smile reminded Drusus of a hungry wolf.

"She is not feeling well, my friend. You have been married before; you know how women can be when the moon is rising."

"I see. I hope that she is up to receiving company again soon. What did she say about our pending marriage, then?"

"She begs time to consider, as your attentions are a surprise to her."

"How can this be so, old friend? I gave her material for a wedding dress and a Tyrrhenian bed cover. I have spoken my intentions to her many times."

"Is that so?" Drusus raised his eyebrows. "She said naught of this to me."

"Your child was so ungrateful that she gave the material to Claudia Felicia Nicia." Stephanus' mouth narrowed to a straight line.

"Did you tell her your intent for the fabrics?"

"Only that she should make a dress to wear to a dinner after the games I sponsored today. And she did not do that."

"I have been told that Nicia is an ungenerous husband; I am sure that she only wanted to do something kind for her childhood friend. Go to, Stephanus. She had no reason to believe that yours was a betrothal gift. We both know that."

"Drusus …"

"My friend, give the girl time. I will make your case to her. She is young yet, and may need some persuasion. Go home, and I will join you for a cup of wine later. Perhaps by then we will have something joyful to toast."

"She makes a fool of herself with this Britannicus, Drusus. He is a conspicuous person, and he has no *dignitas*. He even violates our clothing laws, appearing in a toga to which he is not entitled; I have seen it with my own eyes. I am a law-abiding and successful man, old friend. Surely there is no need to consider Drusilla's wishes; she is young and silly."

"If we want to be technical about things, Stephanus, you have no *dignitas* either. You are also a freedman," Drusus stated. "Now, I ask you again. Please, go home for the moment. I must present your case. My daughter is not foolish. Regardless of what other fathers might do, I would not dispose of her hand without her input."

"Very well. Please, come to my dinner. You will sit at my right hand as an honored guest. I look forward to the day when I may call you father-in-law."

Stephanus took his leave, paying no attention to the immaculately dressed man on the client bench outside the door. As soon as Felix was certain Stephanus was long gone, he admitted Suetonius to the atrium and announced him at the *tablinum* door.

Drusus had to look up to meet the steady green-eyed gaze of his daughter's other suitor. Suetonious was immaculately arrayed in a white tunic and chalked toga, with heavy gold bracelets around his wrists. His black hair, damp from the bath, lay in waves, and the vague scent of myrrh hung about him.

Myrrh for her courses, indeed.

Drusus would deal with Claudia and Drusilla's deception later; he now knew with whom his daughter had been keeping company in the baths even as he arrived. The man certainly made an impression.

Suetonius extended his hand, and the two men gripped each other's forearms.

"*Ave*, Marcus Suetonius," Drusus said, as though it were his own office into which the other man had entered. "You need no introduction."

"*Salve*, Drusus Gaius. My apologies for not coming during visiting hours, or requesting an appointment. I understand that you have only just returned to town, and so I made haste. I have come to speak to you of your daughter."

"So I gathered from my conversation with her. Tell me, how will you care for her should I agree to your suit? You have a competitor in Stephanus, who is a successful businessman."

"I have put aside funds from my purses these many years, with an eye to purchasing a home. Whether it be in my native Britain, I cannot say; I have long been away from there. I am minded to find a place in Neapolis, but if it would better suit Drusilla I could look here. If she would prefer, we could even to go Oplontis, or Rome."

"Oplontis! You would rub elbows with the wealthiest folk of all, then?" Drusus smiled. "Let us be frank with one another, Suetonius. Drusilla's dowry will be modest at best. I am looking to establish a new household with a woman in Herculaneum and must take that into consideration as well."

"Since we are being frank with one another, Drusus, I will tell you that I would wish for Drusilla's hand even if she came with nothing but the clothes on her back. Your daughter is an extraordinary woman."

"I have much to think on, Suetonius. Perhaps you will call on me again tomorrow, that we might talk further."

Suetonius was grateful that his voice didn't quaver and his knees didn't knock. He'd never pursued marriage before; only a woman like Drusilla could have inspired him.

They said their goodbyes and Drusus watched Suetonius walk out of the house. The gladiator's clothing was of a finer quality than his own, even the forbidden toga, and he had certainly made at least a small case for himself. The gold around the man's wrists was worth a fortune. There was also the matter that Drusilla had made her preferences well known, but that had to be weighed against the debts he owed Stephanus.

Maybe Suetonius would pay those debts on my behalf. No, that will never happen. But I might be able to persuade him to make a loan ... No.

The only thing that made sense right now was to delay making the decision and hope that his strong-willed daughter could be persuaded to accept the fuller.

Drusus changed into his finest clothes to attend Stephanus' dinner. He walked the few blocks to the fuller's house alone. He hoped to string the wealthy man along a little bit longer with the coins in his purse, a partial payment on the debt he had owed for so many years.

One of Stephanus' female slaves greeted him after he gave his name to the door keeper. Her black hair was bound back in a tight braid down her back, and she wore a simple woolen tunic. A pendant around her neck declared her Stephanus' property and guaranteed a reward to anyone who caught her if she ran away.

"I am assigned to you for the evening," she said, her eyes downcast. "My master bids me do as you wish in all matters."

"What is your name?"

"My master calls me Livilla."

"And what did your family call you?"

"Arsinoë."

An Egyptian slave! What a fashionable coup for Stephanus.

"Are you his bed girl?"

She nodded, her shame evident in her bearing.

"Your master is generous indeed, then."

"The dinner is taking place in the garden." Livilla led the way past the fullery and into the peristyle. Several couches and tables had been arranged for a large party of Stephanus' clients.

"Ah, Drusus! I see you have met Livilla. I hope that you find her … satisfactory."

"I will wish to discuss some business with you after supper, old friend. And I hope that you will find our discussions equally … satisfactory."

"Come, old friend, and share this couch with me. Livilla will wash your feet. Then, we must drink to … business."

At dinner, Stephanus plied Drusus with the choicest bits of food and fine Falernian wine.

"I wish to make a clean breast of things, old friend," Stephanus said as he ordered Drusus' cup filled with more wine. "I wish to marry your daughter. I know I am old, but I will make her a fine husband. Confidentially, I do not wish to keep dying my hair with these concoctions to look younger; I would think that an older, established man would be a desirable match. We could even talk of favorable financial terms for you rather than a dowry. What say you, old friend?"

Drusus hiccuped a little and took another swallow of wine. "I suppose you could always wear a wig."

Stephanus laughed as he cast his eye toward Livilla's black braid.

Chapter 27

Pompeii

Eight days after the Ides of August, 79 CE

Drusus and Stephanus concluded their negotiations with a handshake, then Drusus sent for his daughter. Drusilla refused to look at Stephanus, who appeared overly pleased with himself.

"I will make you a bargain, daughter. Send to your Suetonius and ask him to meet you here at the sixth hour on the twenty-fifth day of the month. We will array you in your bridal attire. Should he appear, I will allow this marriage. If he does not appear, you must marry Stephanus."

"I have every faith in Suetonius; I will send to him." She went to her room to write the message.

Stephanus grinned. '"Drusus, you won't regret this."

"I mislike that smile, old friend."

"I will arrange matters to our mutual liking, Drusus. You have my word."

"By the way, that's a very fine wig you wear."

Stephanus preened. "Indeed. You will find my bed girl, Livilla, the lighter for her shearing. It is fortunate that she is so beautiful;

even with her hair cut like a boy's she is desirable. And I have two new wigs to show for it."

CHAPTER 28

POMPEII

NINE DAYS AFTER THE IDES OF AUGUST, 79 CE

"Britannicus, let me walk with you. We will speak, freedman to freedman. I understand that you have made a proposal of marriage to Drusus Gaius' daughter." Stephanus' smile did not quite reach his eyes.

"My name is Suetonius."

"Really, that's neither here nor there. I have approached Drusus about his daughter, and she has refused me, saying that she is already engaged. I would put a bargain to you. Drusilla has sent you a message asking you to be at her father's home at the sixth hour tomorrow, yes?" He adjusted his black wig, which kept slipping in the heat.

"Yes, she has.'

"I think we should let her dispose of her hand as she sees fit, don't you? If she chooses you, I will let her go to you. However, you must agree not to come yourself."

"And if I do not agree?"

The two were very near the *quadriporticus*, where the *lanista*, Valerius, stood with a grim expression.

"Your patron is going to chain you to the wall, Britannicus. If Drusilla chooses you, she will come to you with the key.'

Suetonius protested. "How do I know you speak true?"

"You have my word as a Roman citizen."

"But you are not a Roman citizen, Stephanus."

"My word as a fellow freedman, then. Besides, surely you do not doubt Drusilla."

Suetonius removed one of his bracelets and allowed himself to be shackled to the wall. The *lanista* gave the key, which was part of a ring, to Stephanus. Valerius had been paid well for his part in the stratagem.

"What if she chooses you?" Suetonius thought it unlikely.

"I'll send a slave to have you unlocked. After all, I'll be busy celebrating my marriage." Stephanus' laugh was unpleasant.

Stephanus gave Valerius a bag of coins and turned to leave the barracks. Before doing so, he picked up Suetonius' bracelet and slipped it over his arm.

"Drusilla appears to prefer her men bedecked; it behooves me to dress appropriately for our wedding."

With that, he walked out the door. On the way back to the fullery, he slipped the ring onto his little finger, the tines faced inward so that it looked like an ordinary ornament. The ground rumbled beneath his feet as he did so; Vulcan was at his forge. Stephanus had no intention of revealing the key until after he and Drusilla were married.

The sky darkened.

Valerius picked up his bundle. "I gave the extra key to Hannibal; I do not trust this fuller."

"Then why did you agree to his terms?"

"I need the money." Valerius shrugged. "May the gods smile upon you, Britannicus. You have been a good friend. I am for Oplontis."

"Suetonius."

"What did you say?" Valerius looked back.

"My name, Valerius. It's Suetonius. I've never forgotten."

"Farewell, Suetonius." Valerius walked out of the *quadriporticus* and on to the rock-covered roadway that led out of Pompeii.

For his part, Hannibal was drinking at the Lucky Phoenix. He knew that he should be going back to the barracks to free his friend, for Valerius had told him what was happening. But there was a beautiful Egyptian *lupa* on his knee, and the wine was good. There was plenty of time.

In Nicia's finest bedroom, Claudia had gone into labor. Despite the sweltering heat, she wore her best dress and jewels; providing an heir to the family was an important occasion. Regardless of the fact that Nicia had never touched her, and clearly didn't care about her peccadilloes, the child she brought forth this day would one day receive a great deal of wealth. Nicia and his boon companion, Vorenus, were in the corridor while the midwife and priestess made their chants and preparations.

"Whom do you think is the father," Vorenus asked his lover.

"I don't give a damn," Nicia replied, reaching up to caress Vorenus' shaven scalp. "If I were a wagering man, I'd say it was that Gallic gladiator. The one they call Vercingetorix, after the old king of legend. I've seen her make calf's eyes at him enough times. And her foster sister, Drusilla, is rumored to have taken Britannicus, the Thracian turned *magister ludi,* as a lover; the two women are alike as two peas in a pod. Gladiators' whores. Feh."

The timbers supporting the roof creaked under the weight of the pumice that had rained down on the city for the past twenty-four hours.

"You should go to your wife," Vorenus said, kissing Nicia's cheek. "The forms must be observed."

Nicia caressed Vorenus' cheek in return, took a deep breath, and started to walk away. He turned back and took Vorenus in his arms for a passionate kiss. Smoothing the blue linen robes his companion wore, he smiled. "I never thought anyone would look beautiful without eyebrows. I adore you, Vorenus."

Then, he strode out of the hall and into the nearby room.

"How soon before my son is born?"

Chapter 29

Pompeii

Ten days after the Ides of August, 79 CE

"I don't understand." Drusilla wore a white tunic with a silk cord around the waist. Her *ornatrix* had spent hours braiding her hair into the *seni crines* style and pinning a flower crown over it all before covering her face with a saffron-colored veil. Her eyes were rimmed with kohl, her lids brushed with crushed lapis pigment, and her lips rouged lightly with carmine. The shoulders of her tunic were held together with the peacock brooches, and the faience beads and earrings completed her ensemble. She held a spindle, which she would carry to her new home to represent setting up housekeeping. "Where is Suetonius?"

"Clearly this Brittanicus was trifling with you, Drusilla," Stephanus said, smoothing a lock of his black wig over one ear. "Not too surprising; he's a gladiator, which means he is tainted with *infamia*. No better than a slave, freedman or not. A bargain is a bargain. He is not here at the appointed hour, and he has no legal recourse. You agreed to marry me if he did not appear."

"This cannot be right." Drusilla looked around the atrium again, as though Suetonius might appear from the shadows.

"You will marry Stephanus, as we all agreed. I am still your father, with the right to dispose of your hand," Drusus added.

"I won't. He's as old as you; his son is older than me."

Drusus struck her, hard across the face. Stephanus merely smiled and toyed first with a gold bracelet around his wrist and then a ring on his little finger.

"I appreciate you teaching Drusilla her place so tidily. I don't mind a spirited woman between the bed covers, but a proper Roman woman shouldn't speak like that to her father."

Drusilla slammed the spindle to the ground, breaking the instrument, and shouted at her father while pointing at Stephanus.

"I will not marry him. Ever. I don't know how many times I've told you this. His house stinks of piss from the fullery, and he beats his slaves. He's a cruel master who wants to lord over them, even though he was a slave himself. I want no part of him."

It was then that Drusilla recognized the bracelet around Stephanus' scrawny wrist. It hung loose, being made for a larger man.

"What have you done to Suetonius?" She ground out her words.

Drusus raised his hand again, just as Invictus, who had watched from the corner, launched himself. The elderly dog latched onto Drusus' wrist, sinking his teeth deep into the flesh and tearing.

Seeing her chance, Drusilla ran out of the house. She looked back only long enough to see Invictus sitting on the walkway outside the door as the roof of her father's house caved in.

"Good boy," she called. "Wait for me; I will be back soon." Invictus watched her go.

Drusilla knew she had to get to the gladiator barracks in the *quadriporticus*. She ran through the darkened streets, thanking the gods that she knew her way so well. The pumice was so high in places that it was hard to move, but she had to keep going. She lifted the hem of her *tunica recta* and wrapped the *flammeum* around her throat so that it wouldn't be lost.

She passed a family going the opposite direction, a young husband and wife, with their small daughter. The little girl was barely able to walk; it was obvious that she was not even two years old. Yet, neither parent carried her; they held her hands as she struggled to keep up between them. The adults carried small bundles in their other hands as they hurried over the light stones that covered the road. She was sure she'd seen them in the forum or the market, or even Julia's home; they all looked familiar. Neither she nor the young family exchanged greetings as they made for their destinations.

The next person she saw was Iacobus, walking in the same direction as the young family. She hailed her old tutor, who moved slowly as he used a staff to feel his way along the walk.

"Drusilla Gaia, we must all away. I am for the outer wall near the theatre. You must leave."

Indeed, escape was the only thing on Drusilla's mind: escape with Suetonius.

"I promise you, Iacobus, I will take the *Porta Saliensis*. There is one whom I must find first."

"Your sweetheart," the wise old man nodded. "You were never meant for Stephanus, the gods told me so. You must go now, but be careful. May the gods keep you, Drusilla Gaia. I hope that we are able to meet again one day."

Did everyone know about Stephanus? How could I have been so blind?

The kindly old man gripped her arm gently in farewell, and then proceeded on his way again. Drusilla did the same, walking rapidly rather than running now; the brief stop had made her realize that she was out of breath.

She had just passed Nicia's house when its roof caved in, no longer able to stand the weight of the stones. Drusilla hoped that Claudia was elsewhere; her time to deliver the baby was surely near. There was no time to go back and find out, though; Drusilla had only one task in mind.

At last, she rounded the corner near the theatre and the Odeon. People were carrying their goods on their backs, many with cushions tied to their heads to fend off any further rocks that might fall from the sky.

When she entered the *palaestra*, she cried out for Suetonius. There were a few other people milling around there, and one man finally showed her where he was shackled to the wall. "We've been trying to free him, but we need to look to ourselves, *domina*," was all the explanation she received.

"Thank Mars you're here. Where is the key?" Suetonius was wild-eyed with relief. Perspiration poured from his body; the air in the room was close and hot.

"What key?"

"Stephanus said you would bring the key if you chose me. The key to these shackles; it's a ring lock."

Drusilla recalled Stephanus' smirk as he played with the ring. "He said nothing to me of this. Oh, how I hate him. Is there no other key? Where is Valerius?"

"Valerius is gone; he says he gave the other to Hannibal, but he has not come."

Nor would he; the roof of the Lucky Phoenix had also caved in, trapping all within it.

Drusilla looked around her; there were so many rooms around the *palaestra*; a key could be anywhere. She studied the lock; it was a simple mechanism, not a fancy sickle lock. She pulled two bodkins from her hair, thanking the gods that the *ornatrix* had also sewn the braids together. Remembering how she and Claudia would pick the locks of the food storage cabinet as children, she worked at the device. But her hands shook and she couldn't make the tumblers move.

"I can't open it. Suetonius, I'm frightened." She sat down next to him, wrapping her arms around him, no longer caring about whether her dress was still snowy white or whether she was too warm. The fuller be damned; she would loathe him forever.

"I will always take care of you, my love. You came to me as a bride, Drusilla. When this is over, we will wed in truth. I wish to be with you for the rest of my days. Take my bracelet and wear it, and we will call ourselves married."

"I will be honored to be your wife." She slid his remaining bracelet up her arm and kissed him, just as a horrible explosion rent the air and shook the ground.

Suetonius's beautiful green eyes were the last thing Drusilla saw as the world came to an end.

Chapter 30
Day 10
Later

Stephanie woke, disoriented and screaming, in a room she didn't recognize. An elderly lady in a bright pink blouse, her silver hair pulled back in a black bow that matched her cardigan, sat in a chair next to the bed. Stephanie tried to sit up.

"*Piano, piano*. Slowly, slowly."

"Where am I?" She was wearing an unfamiliar black silk pajama shirt trimmed in scarlet, though she vaguely remembered Damiano bringing some of her things to the hospital. Everything after that was a blur.

"My grandson, Damiano, he brought you to our home. The sun made you sick and you went to the hospital. He brought you here instead of your hotel so that he could look after you. Your things are hanging up to dry after I washed them. I will bring water."

Nonna Maria left the bedroom and Stephanie looked around to get her bearings. Damiano had mentioned that he'd "worked on a painting project" in between teaching classes on-line during the quarantine; this was clearly it. The far wall, the one she faced as she sat up in bed, was painted in shades of ivory, red, gold, and black in what she knew to be the Pompeiian Third Style. The work showed a well-trained and steady hand, and a great deal of care; the photos she'd seen on-line had not adequately captured Damiano's talent and skill.

The rest of the walls were ivory, with photographs and small prints hanging on them. The bed was wide and comfortable, but she still pushed herself into a seated position to get out.

Nonna Maria returned with a glass of ice water. "You drink slowly, *si*? *Piano, piano*, slowly, slowly. Do not be concerned for the bad dreams; you are safe now. What did you dream?"

"I was trapped in a building when Vesuvius erupted. I was with someone I loved, and I wouldn't leave him. I have always been afraid of being trapped in a small space …" Stephanie' voice trailed off.

Nonna Maria took her hand and squeezed it; the elderly lady's grip was strong and comforting. "As I said, you are safe here. I will let my grandson know you are awake."

"Where is he?"

"Stirring the risotto. He wanted to make sure you had something good to eat when you woke up."

Stephanie sipped at her water as she watched *Nonna* Maria walk out again. She felt tired, and embarrassed to have fainted at Pompeii, let alone screaming herself awake from the worst night terror she'd ever experienced. How could she possibly tell Damiano about it?

As suddenly as she thought of him, Damiano stood in the door with a tray.

"*Principessa*. Do you want to try to eat?"

"I hear you made risotto; how can I resist?"

He put the tray on the bedside table and pulled a chair over. "Do you need help to stand?"

"I'm fine."

"Perhaps you'll humor me and let me assist you?"

She smiled, and let him help her from bed to the chair. She took a bite of the sumptuous dish, its creaminess offset by a hint of lime juice and some beautiful shrimp.

"It's delicious, Damiano."

She didn't speak again until she'd finished the bowl. "Thank you for lending me your pajama shirt. I'm embarrassed that my own nighty was so childish."

"Not a word of it, *principessa*. It made me smile. Nor was it childish; a sense of child-like whimsy should never leave us. Now, if you will allow me, I need to show you something." He helped her stand and led her over to the Third Style wall. "I don't know how well you can see the details in this medallion, but I painted this during the quarantine, long before I met you."

Stephanie leaned forward to get a closer look at the tiny portrait encircled in gold paint, supported on either side by acanthus vines. It was a dark-haired woman with blue eyes, wearing a white dress and a golden veil, set against a red background. In tiny golden capital letters around one edge, as though it were a coin face, it read Drusilla Gaia Suetonia. The face was clearly her own.

Stephanie trembled, and Damiano hurriedly helped her back toward the bed so she could sit down. He closed the bedroom door and sat down next to her.

"Damiano, remember that day in Naples when I told you that I had reason to believe no one could understand who I am? I need to tell you about the dreams I had after I fainted."

To her astonishment, Damiano didn't bat an eye at the fabulous tale.

"I think we were meant to be together," he whispered when she finished her story. He put his arms around her and kissed her throat.

Stephanie angled her mouth to catch his; Damiano slid his tongue between her teeth. When he leaned her back on the bed. Stephanie made no objection.

"How I have wanted to make love to you, *principessa*. It has been so difficult to wait, but I don't want to delay any longer. Please, will you let me love you?"

"I have never wanted a man in my life the way I want you."

Stephanie worked at the buttons of the pajama shirt while Dom stripped off his shirt and jeans. He joined her on the bed and the two slid between the sheets. Dom pressed her breasts together so that both nipples fit in his mouth while Stephanie entwined her fingers in his raven-black hair. Their hips moved in rhythm, even as Dom slipped her panties away and dropped them off the edge of the bed.

He kissed his way down her belly to the dark curls below, dividing them tidily with his fingers to find her pleasure center. He caressed it gently with his thumb as he slipped his tongue inside her. Then, one finger went where his tongue had gone and he wrapped his lips around the tiny button. Stephanie's hips bucked with ecstasy as he lapped at her sex, preparing her to receive him.

When she was right at the edge, Dom took her hand and guided it to her wetness.

"Touch yourself, Stephanie," he whispered as he pulled a condom from a nearby drawer. "Let me watch you."

He slipped the latex over his hard length, never taking his eyes from Stephanie as she caressed herself.

"Now, guide me."

Stephanie caressed his velvety hardness; Dom quivered as she helped him slide the whole length into her.

It took a moment for them to find their rhythm again, but soon they moved as one.

"You feel so good to me, Stephanie." His breath was hot on her ear.

He whispered "*Sono tua*," over and over again as they moved together. *I am yours*.

Her internal muscles fluttered and Dom groaned. "If you do that again, I will not be able to control myself."

"I don't want you to control yourself. I am so very close to …"

Dom slipped a hand between them and fingered her as he thrust harder and deeper.

"Say my name, *principessa*," he growled as she came.

"Suetonius. Damiano. Magister." She purred into his ear as he shuddered with his own climax. "Mi amor."

The last slipped out before Stephanie had a moment to think about what she'd said. Damiano didn't respond beyond kissing her deeply and making sure she was comfortable. She was asleep before he returned to bed after disposing of the prophylactic.

"*Buona notte, mi amor*," he whispered in her ear as he settled in next to her, drifting off with his arm draped across her shoulders.

"*Principessa*, I want to talk to you about this book I read to you in the hospital. Maybe it is none of my business; after all, I am still the little boy who got lost in stories of vengeful gods and goddesses. But I worry that maybe it was not such a healthy thing for you."

Stephanie put her hand over his. "Dom, I read books like that because real life doesn't always work out the way it does in books. In thrillers and mysteries, the villains are alway brought to justice. In romance, the two protagonists always live happily ever after."

Her smile was wistful. "Sometimes, it happens in real life, sure. But most of the time it doesn't. Most of the time, the bad guys get away with it. Or someone has to leave the person they want to be with, for any number of reasons. In those books, I can live vicariously and know that it will all work out in the end."

Stephanie looked away, hoping Dom hadn't seen the tears in her eyes. They had only a few days remaining, and she didn't want to leave.

Chapter 31

Day 13

Damiano handed her a gift bag and sat down on the hotel bed. "Please, open it now. I wanted to make sure you had these things to take with you."

In the bag were some Italian goodies, like ginger mint toothpaste. A red coral *cornicello*, the Neapolitan good luck charm, on a chain that Dom fastened around her neck. A souvenir ring from the Naples Archaeological Museum, a replica of a ring found at Pompeii. It was small and meant for a child, but Damiano put it on her little finger, where it fit beautifully. Finally, there were was a tiny bottle of Italian perfume; it smelled of jasmine and spice.

"Each night, *principessa*, I want you to use this before you go to bed. I hope that the jewelry and fragrance will remind you of me, and the short time we had together."

"I almost wish I didn't have to go home, Dom." She put the perfume and toothpaste back in the bag and tucked it into her suitcase. "I am going to miss you."

"If nothing else, the pandemic taught us that we can keep in touch with friends far away." He took her hand, and brushed his lips across her knuckles, just as he had the day they met. Had it really only been two weeks ago?

"And, of course, those who are more than friends."

Neither of them dared speak of love again.

Stephanie called Raylene that night.

"Raye, I am so confused. I honestly think I'm in love with Damiano, which is completely ridiculous. I've only known the man for a couple of weeks. It would never work anyway."

"What makes you say that? Stranger things have happened. Unless, of course, you're trying to talk yourself out of something. Is that it?"

"For god's sake, Raye, he wears silk pajamas. My bathrobe has animal ears on the hood. He's so far out of my league that it's ridiculous."

"First, you rock that robe. And second, how do you know he wears silk pajamas?"

"I woke up wearing the top half of them while his grandmother washed the things I had at the hospital. That's not the point."

"Let me ask you something, Steph. Has he kissed you?"

"Several times."

"Did you like it?"

"Yeah …"

"Did you make love?"

"It was incredible. But he could have just been having a little spring break fling of his own."

"You don't believe that. I can tell by the tone of your voice."

"I don't know what to think, Raye. Dom is the most amazing man I've ever met. I don't want to leave. But I have my life and he has his. He's talking about staying in touch, but … Raye, I'm scared."

"Steph, if you really like him, take a leap of faith. He could be the one."

CHAPTER 32

DAY 14

Far too soon, Damiano was helping Stephanie with her bags outside the Naples airport. He kissed her goodbye and watched her as she walked through the sliding doors in the early morning darkness.

"Until we meet again, my love," he whispered before turning his car toward the road the led back to Pompei.

CHAPTER 33

THE FOLLOWING MONTHS

Maintaining a long-distance relationship turned out to be harder than they'd thought. The nine-hour time difference meant that they were seldom able to connect on FaceTime or Zoom without one of them being exhausted, so they turned to increasingly wistful e-mails, and often included links to music videos that spoke words with which they struggled themselves.

When *Time Away* sent Stephanie to Barcelona a couple of months later, Dom met her there and stayed for a couple of days. They whiled away hours in a hotel with windows shaped like palm trees, content to simply hold one another, and had a beautiful dinner on Montjuic, with views of the entire city below them.

The time felt entirely too brief; soon it was back to videos and e-mails.

The morning that Stephanie woke up to find a link to the Mamas & Papas' version of "Dedicated to the One I Love" in her e-mail box, she burst into tears. Outside that impassioned utterance the night they first made love, so far as Stephanie knew, neither of them had mentioned love. Still, she knew her heart and what she felt for Damiano, even with so many obstacles to overcome.

She wrote a lengthy e-mail and, at the end, tapped out a "Ti amo" in response to his video and went to have a good cry in the shower. It was past time to admit the truth of her feelings.

Dom glanced at his phone before joining his grandmother for dinner in his cousin's restaurant. He re-read the e-mail several times before Stephanie's words finally sank in. He had worried about sending that song to her: that he was saying too much, too soon. Apparently not; the words they'd said after making love that first time were real … even if neither was sure the other had heard.

"My dearest Dom:

I recently read a beautiful book. Bear with me while I tell you about it, because at first it won't make sense. The main character is miserable in her life and so she tries to kill herself. She winds up in a special place, where a woman who had been one of her mentors helps her look not only at her regrets, but at the lives she might have chosen other than the one she did. She gets to see what all of her different dreams would have looked like … but some of them make her wonder what else she might have imagined.

And that's the thing: I never imagined how my life would change by visiting a small town on the other side of the world. I never imagined that I would find my soul mate, literally, by taking a magazine assignment … one that I almost turned down because I was afraid to leave the house.

I think all the time about what it would have been like if I'd stayed in that place of fear instead of taking a chance.

I never imagined how hard it would be to be apart from you. I feel as though you complete me.

I don't want to try to imagine life without you in it. That's why I'm taking another leap of faith right now.

Ti amo, Damiano De Luca. Sono tua."

It took him only a moment to send a quick e-mail to a former colleague in the United States before he walked out of the house. *Qui audit adipiscitur … he who dares, wins.*

And now would come the hard part.

CHAPTER 34

"*Mille grazie*, Dr. Thomas. Many thanks. I look forward to talking further." Dom hit the "end call" button on his phone and went to talk to *Nonna* Maria about the professorship he'd just accepted.

"*Nonna*, I need to talk to you about something."

"You are finally going after that girl, aren't you, Damià? It's past time."

All he could do was stare.

"I wasn't born yesterday, Damià. I know how a man in love behaves. You've been moping around since you took that young lady to the airport. The only times you are happy are when you have heard from her. And don't you worry about me. I've known this day was coming; your cousin will help me with whatever I need. Besides, now. I can move into that big Roman room of yours and save my room for guests."

Damiano gaped at his grandmother and then recovered his dignity. "*Grazie, Nonna*. It'll be a while before I go; I need to arrange some things first."

"Of course you do, Damiano. You can't propose without a ring. In all seriousness, though, you remember how I told you that your *nonno* was my soulmate? How we knew we were right for each other very quickly? Well, I believe that soulmates are together throughout time, and that they recognize one another. I think that girl is your soulmate. So go get her a ring and go after her."

"There's one more thing I need to get besides a ring, *Nonna*. I think she'll want that more than any jewel I could give her. I need to go over to the archaeological site."

CHAPTER 35

SIX MONTHS AFTER LEAVING POMPEI

Stephanie turned down her iTunes, which was playing one of her favorite songs, and stared out her office window. The slouchy tan pullover she'd bought in Naples slipped off of one shoulder; she'd hitched it up repeatedly and decided to just leave it. She'd slipped her flats off under the desk, so her feet were bare below her jeans. She played with the ring around her right pinky, twisting it back and forth as the light hit the blue stone in its pewter setting. The red *cornicello* necklace finished her ensemble; she'd worn both every day since Damiano gave them to her. Anyone who knew Stephanie would have been able to tell her mind was not on her latest assignment.

The phone rang and she answered it absently. "Time Away, this is Stephanie."

"Miss Marlowe, there's a package for you here in the lobby. It's from Pompei. Do you want to come and get it or should I bring it up?" Raylene sounded amused. She had fit right in when the office re-opened and the magazine needed a receptionist.

"I'm on deadline. Could you do me a huge favor and bring it up? I'd come down but I'm really in the flow and want to finish this up. You know how it goes. And please, just call me Stephanie … yes, even when we're at work." Stephanie hated lying to Raylene; she hadn't been able to focus all day.

"Okay. I'll be up in a minute."

Stephanie turned back to her laptop but found herself looking out the window again instead of at the article she was writing. She still couldn't make sense of Damiano's e-mail from two weeks ago.

"You left some things in Pompei. Where should I have them delivered?"

She hadn't noticed anything missing in the six months since her return and had no idea what Dom was talking about. She'd given him the office address, so this had to be it. Leaving packages at her place with no one to receive them just meant a notice from the post office.

She heard the door open behind her. "Leave it on the desk, please."

She was about to turn around when a cold nose butted her hand. She looked down to see the black and tan mutt she'd fallen in love with in the Pompeii ruins, wagging his tail furiously.

"Buon-cane!" She hugged his neck and kissed the top of his head. "Or maybe I should call you Invictus." The dog wagged his tail even harder.

"I hope I am as welcome. You look beautiful, my *principessa*." Damiano leaned against the doorframe. His hair was longer, with a soft wave of fringe across his forehead, and the stubble on his jaw was so even that it had to be a choice rather than a missed shave. He wore a dark jacket over snug jeans and a pale green shirt, looking every inch the college professor. The gladiator had disappeared inside the scholar once again, and Stephanie had never seen anything so beautiful as his smile at that moment.

"Oh, my God." Stephanie started to cry.

"I couldn't stop thinking of you, and e-mail was just not enough," he said as he walked over to her desk. "I even adopted 'your' dog, so I could bring him to you. I hope, my love, that you will have both us. *Negabit mi tibi, Drusilla*?"

He was in front of her on one knee, his meaning unmistakable as he took her hands in his. Still, he asked again. "Stephanie Marlowe, *la mia principessa, te sposarmi*? Will you marry me?"

He took a box from his jacket pocket and opened it to reveal a platinum ring set with a sapphire; the adult-sized twin of the souvenir ring he'd given her months ago.

"But your job … and I'm not even wearing shoes! Dom …"

"I start teaching classics at San Francisco State University next semester; they were delighted to add an expert on Pompeii to their masters curriculum," he replied. "I have seen your beautiful bare feet before. And you didn't answer my question."

Stephanie thought for a moment, making sure she had the right words. "*I uxorum ducere*, Suetonius. *Io soposeró te*. I will be your wife, my dearest love. My gladiator."

The only sound that could be heard as they kissed was Buon-Cane's tail thumping happily on the floor, watching a reunion he'd expected for centuries.

Acknowledgments

I started writing this book in the days just before the world-wide shelter-in-place due to COVID-19. Like many people dealing with the ambient trauma of the lockdown, I struggled creatively. I had problems with a first draft that I genuinely believed would be finished by year's end, as I tried to imagine how a romance in a post-COVID world might work. That's why you see references to the pandemic and how we all tried to muddle through.

The hardest blow of a difficult 2020 came on December 20, when one of my dearest friends died after six months in hospital for a non-COVID illness. It is to him that this book is dedicated; Iacobus, the tutor, is named after him.

I eventually set this work aside and completed another project before coming back to it. In a supreme irony, I began the finishing touches in 2023 when, despite having had five vaccines, I acquired the virus myself during a writing conference. It was then that I decided to release the book as a novella.

New research has frequently come to light since my visit to Pompeii, Naples and Herculaneum. I made use of it in the text where I could. All of the characters in ancient Pompeii have their basis in remains found at the sites.

There is now some controversy about the date of the eruption, with some researchers believing that the traditional August date is based on a mistranslation of Pliny the Younger's letters. They believe the eruption may have occurred in October. I have chosen to use the traditional August date in this story.

Throughout this pandemic, I have worried more than I care to admit about the people whom I met during my all-to-brief sojourn in Campania.

Thanks to: Daniela Mantice and Andante Travels. The staffs of La Vinicola, Ristorante Zi' Caterina, and Hotel Palma for great food and lodging, as well as their generosity. The towns of Pompei and Ercolano, where everyone was so nice. The wonderful new friends I made along the way, especially Steve and Wendy. Otto, for driving us from Naples Airport to Pompeii and back. Duolingo for refreshing my Italian language skills and helping me learn Latin.

To Gregory S. Aldrete, PhD, Darius Arya, PhD, Mary Beard, PhD, Laura Benitti, Bettany Hughes, PhD, David Soren, PhD, Steven L. Tuck, PhD, Matthew Nichols, PhD, Livia Galante, Fiorella Squillante, Danielle Oteri, Stephen Saylor, and food historian Francine Segan, whose books, courses, and documentaries brought the ancient world to life for me.

To novelist Ken Gire, whose excellent *Centurion* had a number of reference excerpts in the end notes. The excerpts from an 1872 book entitled *Adam's Roman Antiquities* were particularly useful in identifying job titles in the ancient Roman world. As the book is long out of print, I am grateful to Mr. Gire for his thoroughness. Thanks to Matt Haig, whose stunningly beautiful *The Midnight Library* is referenced in Stephanie's e-mail to Dom.

Quotations from Ovid and Lucretius are in the public domain.

Two Requests

If you enjoyed this book, please leave a review on your favorite site. Independent authors like me depend on your kind word-of-mouth to help us reach a wider audience and find new readers.

Finally, I would love it if you would join my mailing list. You'll get a free short story just for registering. I promise you wont't be spammed, and that your information will never be sold.

Sign up here: http://eepurl.com/dcPS31

Thank you.

Glossary

Aedile: Entry-level Roman magistrate

As: Unit of Roman coinage

Ave: Hail/Be well

Buon cane: Good dog

Buongiorno: Good morning

Buonna notte: Good night

Caldarium: Hot tub in the bath house

Calamistrum: Heated curling iron

Campania: the region of Italy that contains Pompeii, Herculaneum, and Naples

Cena libera: A formal dinner hosted before a series of gladiatorial games. Wealthy guests would come to watch gladiators eat what could be their last meal.

Cornicello: A small carved horn, usually made of red coral. A Companion good luck charm.

Cornu: Large, curved trumpet

Dignitas: dignity and gravitas, considered an essential quality of Roman manhood which only freeborn citizens could obtain

Domina: Lady/Mistress

Dominus: Lord/Master

Editor: Sponsor of gladiatorial games

Equites: Originally, members of the Roman cavalry. Later, an elite political group.

Faience: Glazed ceramic ware, usually the color of turquoise

Fare bella figura: A woman who makes a good impression

Fibulae: Decorative pins used by Roman women to hold their dresses together at the shoulder

Flammeum: Roman wedding veil, typically gold or orange

Frigidarium: Cold plunge pool in the bath house

Fullonica: The fullery, where clothes were cleaned and dyed

Garum: Roman fish sauce

Hypocaust: Under-floor heating system, found in many wealthy Roman households

Ides: 15th day of the month in the Roman calendar

Infamia: Infamy. Certain classes of people were considered infamous, including gladiators and slaves, and were not eligible for Roman citizenship.

Insula: Apartment

Kalends: First day of the month in the Roman calendar

La mia donna: My lady

Lanista: Owner/trainer of gladiators

Lares: Household/family gods

Librus: "Freed man," a name often added to their own by former slaves

Lorica segmentata: Segmented leather armor, worn by the Roman military in some periods

Ludus: School, also used in reference to gladiator training camps

Lupa: She-wolf, slang term for a prostitute

Mycelium: Marketplace

Magister ludi: Literally, the master of the schools. Usually the gladiators' physician

Meilichia: Nickname meaning "sweet as honey"

Mille grazie: A thousand thanks

Murmillo: A class of gladiator, one of the heavy fighters.

Negabit mi tibi: Will you marry me?

Nonna: Grandmother

Odeon: Music hall

Ornatrix: Hairdresser

Palaestra: Public area dedicated to teaching sports

Palla: Traditional garment worn by married Roman women, draped in a similar fashion to the toga

Pallium: Roman mantle

Pasta alla genovese: Pasta dish made with beef and onions, a regional specialty

Pater: Father

Pater familias: Head of household

Pecuniam: Purse

Peristyle garden: A garden surrounded by columns, usually next to a veranda or porch

Pizza rustico: Thick-crust pizza with marinara and cheese, invented in Naples

Posca: Vinegar mixed with wine. A version consumed by the gladiators also contained ash from cook fires; modern archaeologists believe that this improved their skeletal strength.

Porta Saliensis: Literally, the salt gate. This was the road that led to the sea prior to Vesuvius' eruption

Praedia: A large villa

Praenomen: First name, generally used only by close family members

Primum pilus: Literally, first spear. An officer in the Roman army

Principessa: Princess

Pseudolas: A comedic play by Plautus

Puls: Bean and barley porridge, the most frequent meal of gladiators

Quadriporticus: Literally, four doors. An outdoor reception area for the theatre and odeon, it was temporarily converted to gladiator barracks in Pompeii.

Quod memoratur, vivit - What is remembered, lives

Rudis: An engraved wooden sword, marked with a gladiator's name and a declaration that he was a free man

Salve: Hail/Welcome

Sanctum: The inner temple

Seni crines: The six-braided hairstyle worn by Vestal Virgins and Roman brides

Sesterce: Unit of Roman coinage

Signore: sir/mister

Signorina: miss/young woman

Signora: madame/older woman

Stola: Woman's overdress

Strigil: A curved blade, used in the bath house to remove oil and perspiration before entering the pools

Tablinum: Office space

Tartufo: A chocolate and cherry ice cream dish, popular in southern Italy

Thermopolium/thermopolia: A walk-up stand where hot food was sold

Thraex: Thracian. A class of gladiator, one of the heavy fighters.

Tonsor: Barber

Triclinium: Formal dining room, with couches for diners to recline

Tunica recta: A white woolen gown with a knotted sash, traditionally worn for Roman weddings

Via Bartolo Lungo: The main street in Pompei, named after a local philanthropist

Sources Consulted While Writing This Book

Books & Periodicals

Abatino, E., De Franciscis, A., Brangantini, I. - *Pompeii & Herculaneum: In the Shadow of Vesuvius, with Reconstructions*

Antiqua, Ancient Numismatics, Catalogue XVII

Beard, Mary - *Pompeii*

Berry, Joanne - *The Complete Pompeii*

Bonetto, Christian, & Sainsbury, Brendan - *Lonely Planet Naples, Pompeii, & the Amalfi Coast*

Cappelli, Rosanna, LoMonco, Annalisa - *National Archaeological Museum of Naples Guidebook*

Casson, Lionel - *Life in Ancient Rome*

Clayton, Matt - *History of Rome: A Captivating Guide*

Clayton, Matt - *Pompeii: A Captivating Guide*

Converso, Claudia - *Treasures of Italy: Herculaneum & Oplantis, Civilization, Art and History*

Curry, Andrew et al - National Geographic, August 2021: *Gladiators: Rome's Original Fight Club*

DK Eyewitness Top 10 Naples and the Amalfi Coast

Faas, Patrick - *Around the Roman Table: Food and Feasting in Ancient Rome*

Grainger, Sally - *Cooking Apicius*

Greenblatt, Stephen - *The Swerve: How the World Became Modern*

Hadas, Moses - *Imperial Rome*

Kleiner, Diana E.E. - *Roman Architecture: A Visual Guide*

Knapp, Robert - *Invisible Romans*

Linn, Jason - *The Dark Side of Rome: A Social History of Nighttime in Ancient Rome*

Made in Pompei magazine

McElduff, Siobhán - *Spectacles in the Roman World*

Potter, T.W. - *Roman Britain*

Roma Numismatics, Auction IV Catalog, 30 Sep 2012

Roma Numismatics & LAC, Auction IV Catalog, 30 Sep - 1 Oct 2012

Ricotti, Eugenia Salza Prima - *Dining As A Roman Emperor*

Soren, David - *Art & Archaeology of Ancient Rome, Vol. 1*

Southon, Emma - *A Fatal Thing Happened on the Way to the Forum*

Steves, Rick - *Snapshot: Naples & The Amalfi Coast, Including Pompeii, Fifth Edition*

Steves, Rick - *Italian Phrase Book & Dictionary*

Trafford, L.J. - *How to Survive in Ancient Rome*

Trafford, L.J. - *Sex and Sexuality in Ancient Rome*

Television/Video Documentaries

British Museum: Pompeii Live
The Celts: Blood, Iron & Sacrifice
Cities of the Underworld: Beneath Vesuvius
Colosseum: The Whole Story
Drinking History: Gladiator Gatorade
Eight Days That Made Rome
Empire Games - Rome: Born in Blood
Great Civilizations of the World: Pompeii
Herculaneum Scrolls: Unraveling History
The Hidden History of Rome
History Imagined: Roman Makeup
Italy's Invisible Cities: Naples
The Last Days of Pompeii
Laura McKenzie's Traveler: The Amalfi Coast
Lost City of Gladiators
Meet the Romans
Meet the Romans: Street Life
Meet the Romans: Behind Closed Doors
National Geographic: Lost Treasures of Rome
The Other Pompeii: Life and Death in Herculaneum
Pompeii: Disaster Street
Pompeii - The Last Day
Pompeii: Life & Death in a Roman Town
Pompeii: The Mystery of the People Frozen in Time
Pompeii: Secrets of the Dead The Real Spartacus
Reconstructing Rome

Rick Steves' Europe: The Amalfi Coast Rick Steves' Europe: Naples and Pompeii

Roman Empire, Seasons 1-3

Rome: Empire Without Limit

Rome: The World's First Super Power

Taste of Travel: Sorrento

Tasting History: The Bread of Ancient Rome: Pompeii's Panis Quadratus

Tasting History: I Finally Made Garum: Ancient Rome's Favorite Condiment

Tasting History: Parthian Chicken

Tasting History: Roman Puls

Weird History: What It Was Like to be a Roman Gladiator

Weird History: What It Was Like to be a Roman Slave

Courses and Seminars

Ancient Roman Househunters International: Luxury Villas of Southern Italy - ContextLearning.com

Archaeocon 2022 - Archaeology Institute of America

Christmas in Italy: Stories and Traditions - ContextLearning.com

Gladiators in Ancient Rome: Blood and Arena - ContextLearning.com

Herculaneum: An Ancient City Preserved - ContextLearning.com

Historical Fiction: An End-Result of Archaeology - Archaeological Institute of America

A Historian Goes to the Movies: Ancient Rome - The Great Courses

Introduction to the Roman Empire - Centre of Excellence

Latin for Beginners - Centre of Excellence

Pompeii: Daily Life in an Ancient Roman City - The Great Courses

Pompeii Uncovered: From Daily Life to Disaster - ContextLearning.com

The Rise of Rome - The Great Courses

Roman Architecture - Yale University, via coursera.org

Roman Art and Archaeology - University of Arizona, via coursera.org

The Roman Empire: From Augustus to the Fall of Rome - The Great Courses

Rome - University of Reading, via FutureLearn

Traveling the Roman Empire - The Great Courses

www.ingramcontent.com/pod-product-compliance
Ingram Content Group UK Ltd.
Pitfield, Milton Keynes, MK11 3LW, UK
UKHW041829200726
13854UKWH00002BA/890